B2 11/17
B4

D0994810

SPECIAL MESSAGE TO READERS

THE ULVERSCROFT FOUNDATION
(registered UK charity number 264873)
was established in 1972 to provide funds for research, diagnosis and treatment of eye diseases. Examples of major projects funded by the Ulverscroft Foundation are:-

- The Children's Eye Unit at Moorfields Eye Hospital, London
- The Ulverscroft Children's Eye Unit at Great Ormond Street Hospital for Sick Children
- Funding research into eye diseases and treatment at the Department of Ophthalmology, University of Leicester
- The Ulverscroft Vision Research Group, Institute of Child Health
- Twin operating theatres at the Western Ophthalmic Hospital, London
- The Chair of Ophthalmology at the Royal Australian College of Ophthalmologists

You can help further the work of the Foundation by making a donation or leaving a legacy. Every contribution is gratefully received. If you would like to help support the Foundation or require further information, please contact:

THE ULVERSCROFT FOUNDATION
The Green, Bradgate Road, Anstey
Leicester LE7 7FU, England
Tel: (0116) 236 4325
website: www.foundation.ulverscroft.com

TERROR STALKS BY NIGHT

Terror Stalks by Night: When the mutilated corpse of old Lucille Rivers is found lying in her decrepit mansion, Rivers End, the damage appears to be the work of the razor-sharp claw of some monstrous animal. One week later, the remaining members of the Rivers family gather at Rivers End to listen to the reading of the will — but one by one they are systematically slaughtered! While in *Phantom of Charnel House*, a grisly apparition prowls the newly built Charnel Estate, bringing hideous death to all it encounters . . .

Books by Norman Firth
in the Linford Mystery Library:

WHEN SHALL I SLEEP AGAIN?
CONCERTO FOR FEAR
THE LITTLE GREY MAN
THE MODEL MURDERS
FIND THE LADY
BLOOD ON THE DRAGON
TERROR STRIKES
MURDER AT ST. MARK'S
NEMESIS
SONS OF THE SPHINX
INTO THE NIGHT

NORMAN FIRTH

TERROR STALKS BY NIGHT

Complete and Unabridged

LINFORD
Leicester

First published in Great Britain

First Linford Edition
published 2017

Copyright © 1946 by Norman Firth
Copyright © 2016 by Sheila Ings
All rights reserved

*A catalogue record for this book is available
from the British Library.*

ISBN 978–1–4448–3202–0

Published by
F. A. Thorpe (Publishing)
Anstey, Leicestershire

Set by Words & Graphics Ltd.
Anstey, Leicestershire
Printed and bound in Great Britain by
T. J. International Ltd., Padstow, Cornwall

This book is printed on acid-free paper

Contents

Terror Stalks by Night

1

Rivers End

Vivid flashes of lightning, preceded by rumbling bursts of thunder, illuminated the small, unprepossessing village of Riverton. Hissing sheets of rain tumbled from the smoky sky, splattering onto the glistening cobblestones of the main road, hammering like the rattle of distant machine-gun fire on the roof of Bob Carter's Austin Seven, which was parked outside the small station.

Behind the wheel, Bob yawned and lit a second cigarette. He was bored to tears. He had come to Riverton three days ago for a fortnight's rest away from the hustle of London. Friends and relatives had told him how quiet it was in Riverton. Nothing, they had assured him, ever happened in Riverton.

Peace, sunshine, green fields, the smell of new-mown hay, good country beer, roast beef and new potatoes — just the ideal holiday spot for a man who was sick to the teeth of the usual round of night clubs, restaurants, woman-shows, horror plays, and all the rest of what London called 'entertainment'.

They'd painted Riverton in glowing phrases. Fishing, shooting (if seasonable), rowing on the river, inspecting the old Roman ruins, etc., etc.

They'd told him about everything that Riverton had — all except the rain! The rain, it appeared, was an unusual event in Riverton at this time of year. In spite of which, it showed no sign of ceasing. Consequently, fishing, shooting (if seasonable), rowing on the river, inspecting the old Roman ruins, and etc., etc., were ruled out. All that was left was the roast beef and new potatoes — and since Bob could hardly spend the entire day polishing off platefuls of roast beef and new potatoes, he was bored to tears.

There was nothing to relieve that boredom at his hotel. It was the usual rustic affair, half pub; and at the moment, besides himself, and the landlord and his wife, it housed one other guest: a stout retired colonel with white whiskers, rejoicing in the dubious title of Colonel Blumstead-Carrion. But the colonel, whose army career had grown and prospered in India's sunny climes, was not much in the way of entertainment. His conversation ran to Fuzzy-Wuzzies, the caste system, the night young Willis had fallen downstairs at the officers' ball, and curried mutton and brandy. There was a perpetual look in his eye which indicated he was homesick for India and the sound of the muezzin calling the faithful to prayer. Indeed, Bob had expected him, at any given moment, to produce a prayer mat and give a demonstration.

Rather than sit in the parlour imbibing brandy with the colonel, Bob had got his car out and taken a run round in the rain. Finally, he had parked disconsolately near the local station to smoke a cigarette and reflect on the folly of allowing friends to persuade you to take your holidays in godforsaken holes like Riverton.

It was at this moment that a woman emerged from under the station shelter and hurried towards the car.

'Taxi?' she enquired as she drew near. It was on the tip of Bob's tongue to give a polite negative, when he caught a glimpse of her eyes, nose and mouth. The eyes were big and blue; the nose was small and tilted; the mouth was full and red; and the hair, which peeped out from either side of the hood she wore, was golden.

'Yes, miss,' said Bob with a grin as he pulled the collar of his dark coat further up. 'Where d'you want to go?'

The woman climbed in with a grateful sigh and took off her drenched hood, revealing a pretty face framed by a mass of wavy golden hair. 'Do you know Rivers End?' she asked sweetly.

'I suppose they do, some time,' agreed Bob.

'No — I wasn't asking a riddle, driver. I mean the house called Rivers End.'

''Fraid not,' said Bob.

'Oh! Funny, you not knowing that — it's the biggest place round here. You go along the main road, turn left at the old stables, and keep straight up on the hill. It's the big mansion on the hill top — you can't possibly miss it.'

'Right, miss.' Bob nodded, pressing the starter. The Austin shot forward into the night.

Through the driving mirror Bob was able to see the woman using her powder compact to brighten herself up. With one eye on the road ahead, and one on the mirror, he drove on.

The woman bent down and began to pull her drenched stockings up. The car lurched violently and almost ran into the old stables. '*Damn!*' muttered Bob, wrenching at the wheel.

'When you've finished looking through the mirror, driver,' said his passenger calmly, 'I'll go on pulling my stockings up.'

'Sorry, miss,' chuckled Bob. ''S a habit of mine. Looking in the mirror, I mean. Almost lost me licence through it once or twice, I have. Be surprised at the things I've seen, you would.'

'I dare say,' agreed the woman.

'Remember once, a fat businessman and a woman from the chorus of the Follies got in and ...'

'Spare me the gruesome details,' begged the woman.

'Course, that was when I was in London. Now down here there's very little to see ... except last week when the curate and a member of the ladies' sewing circle —'

'Please! If you don't watch your driving you'll crash!'

'Not me, miss.'

The car was now ascending a steep hill. The narrow road on either side was fringed by deep, waterlogged ditches.

Unable to resist the temptation, Bob stole another glance at the mirror. The woman was still pulling her stockings up, and Bob was treated to a glimpse of a pair of beautiful and shapely legs clad in sheer silk, and a hint of pink.

Then, with a shuddering thud, the Austin's nearside wheels skidded into the ditch, and the car heeled over at a most uncomfortable angle. Bob cut the engine.

'There,' exclaimed the woman. 'I told you so!'

'Your fault,' Bob stated calmly. 'If you will have such a perfect pair of legs and go showing them to poor, hard-working, much-married cab drivers, how can you expect to dodge accidents?'

'Well, of all the cheek ...'

Bob clambered from the car and surveyed the extent of the damage. 'That's torn it,' he said ruefully. 'Never get those wheels clear without a crane or a team of horses.'

'The house isn't much further,' said the woman, joining him in the road. 'Perhaps you'd like to come along and phone from there. You can get a breakdown wagon to come along and pick the cab and yourself up.'

'Fine,' agreed Bob. He locked the car doors and turned to accompany her. She was regarding him rather strangely. 'Anything wrong?'

'You don't look like my idea of a cab driver,' she told him.

Bob grinned. 'I'm not! I'm afraid I owe you an apology. I'm down here on a visit ... holiday, I should say. When you chose to make a cabby out of me, I didn't see why not.'

The woman didn't know whether to be annoyed or amused. 'Do you usually go around doing women favours?'

'Only women like you,' Bob assured her.

She smiled and drew her hood on.

'I thought no self-respecting cab driver would be so interested in my legs,' she smiled. 'Oh, well. I suppose I'm indebted to you for getting me here. If you hadn't helped me, I'd probably have been stuck in the station for ages and ages. My name is Jane Rivers — my aunt, Lucille Rivers, used to own the house up there.'

'Used to?'

'Yes.' A worried frown crossed Jane's face. 'She died last week.'

'Oh, I'm sorry.'

'You needn't be. I hardly knew her at all. What worries me is that she died in rather a funny way.'

'She did? How do you mean, funny?'

'She was torn to pieces — as if by some animal with sharp claws!'

'She w-was?' stuttered Bob. 'Then if I were you I'd keep clear of the house.'

'I can't very well. The family are assembling there tonight for the reading of the will. It contains a clause that says it must be read at Rivers End, and that any member of the family who fails to show up automatically loses his or her share of the estate.'

As she finished speaking, a weird, blood-freezing howl echoed through the rain-drenched night. Jane shuddered and held tightly to Bob's coat. 'W-what was th-that?' she gasped.

'It came from the house.' A vivid flash of lightning outlined the top of the hill and the gaunt old pile that was Rivers End. 'Well,' said Bob shakily, 'on second thought I fancy I'll trot back to the village and get the breakdown wagon myself. I don't want to butt in on your family ...'

'Oh, please! You can't let me walk up there all alone,' said Jane faintly.

'All right, I'll go as far as the house with you. But's that's all, mind!'

2

Only Strangers Die!

Cautiously, Jane and Bob approached the massive bolt-studded door of Rivers End. The house loomed gaunt and forbidding above the weed-ridden untended garden, and merely to look at its grey and dreary solidity sent shivers up and down the spines of the man and the woman.

Bob seized a rusty bell-pull and tugged. There was a metallic screeching as the mechanism went into action; then a sonorous bell pealed a deep-toned mournful dirge within the mansion.

'Now listen,' breathed Bob. 'According to all the novels I ever read, we should hear slithering, stealthy footsteps!'

They listened, and sure enough, the sound of slithering footsteps became audible.

'Now there ought to be a rattle of the door chain ...'

The door chain rattled.

'Now the door opens a few inches and a face peers through!' whispered Bob knowingly.

The door opened a few inches and a face peered through.

And what a face! It resembled nothing on Earth. It was the face of a gargoyle, hewn from grey rock, and somewhat clumsily hewn at that. Epstein could have done no worse. Bob gasped, and Jane's grip on his arm tightened.

Had there been a contest to determine the ugliest face in fact or mythology, the running, in Bob's opinion would have been somewhere as follows:

1. The face before him now.

2. Frankenstein's monster.

3. The Gorgons (complete with snakes). The heads of the three Gorgons, in mythology, were reputed to turn any beholder to stone. Well, this present head had turned Bob to stone. The icy shiver that had been chasing along his backbone spread to the rest of his body. His gaze became transfixed. Jane was similarly affected, and for a minute no one spoke.

Then: 'You are Miss Jane Rivers?' enquired the slate-faced monstrosity in a deep voice.

'Er — y-yes!' stammered Jane.

'I have been expecting you. I am the butler, Ashville.'

He opened the door and stood aside for Jane to enter. Beyond him stretched a long gloomy hall, dimly illuminated by a candelabra at the far end.

'Well,' gulped Bob, 'now that you're safely here, I guess I'll push off . . .'

'Oh, no, please!' cried Jane. 'You can't go — you wouldn't leave me here like this . . .'

Some latent spark of chivalry flared up in Bob's breast. Dearly as he wanted to get away from this business, he had no desire to leave Jane there to face heaven knew what.

'But how on earth can I stay?' he enquired.

'I'm sure Ashville will be able to put you up.' Jane half turned, pleadingly, towards the gaunt butler. He looked uncertain.

'Oh, don't bother, Ashville — after all, perhaps all the rooms are occupied, eh?' queried Bob hopefully.

'No, sir, we have plenty of spare rooms here — it wasn't that I was thinking of. I was more concerned with your own personal well-being, sir.'

'Eh?'

'There is a legend attached to this house. It is said that any person, other than a member of the Rivers family or their servants, who sleeps beneath this roof will meet with a most horrible and violent death.'

'That settles it,' Bob said in a small voice. 'Good night, Miss Rivers.'

'Wait a minute,' Jane said in desperation. 'There's no truth in that silly tale, is there, Ashville?'

'Of course not, miss. Why, only two years ago, Major Ashby stayed with your aunt for a period. Of course, he died shortly afterwards ...'

'He did?' said Bob keenly.

'Yes, sir. Most unfortunate it was. He met a horrible fate while hunting big game in Africa. As a matter of fact, he was torn limb from limb by a lioness, poor fellow. Then there was Mr. Tompkins, the mistress's first lawyer. He stayed here for a night or two ...'

'Did he survive?'

'Unfortunately, no. Of course, it would be silly to attribute his death to the old curse; but nevertheless he was struck by a motor car while leaving the house ... I did not see the body, but I understand it was considerably mutilated, sir.'

'Ah, I see,' stuttered Bob.

Jane said: 'Oh, don't pay any attention to those silly stories. The fact that the others died is just a coincidence ...'

'I know,' said Bob. 'That's what they'll say about me, too, one of these days. And,' he went on, putting his finger on the point and pressing, 'I have no desire to forge another link in an already over-long chain of coincidences.'

'You sure you aren't just afraid?' demanded Jane scornfully.

'You're dead right,' agreed Bob. 'I'm scared stiff! But I'm dashed if I'll allow old rockpuss here to frighten me away. I'm staying!'

'Very well, sir,' leered the butler. 'I will instruct the housekeeper to find you accommodation. But don't forget — I warned you!' And with a cold stare, the butler shuffled away down the hall.

Bob gave Jane a sickly grin. 'What do we do now?'

'I don't know. It looks as if we have to find our own way about from here on. I'm afraid Ashville doesn't do his job properly.'

Curiously, they began to walk down the long dismal hall, past stately glimmering suits of armour and a row of oil portraits.

'Who're the whiskery johnnies?' asked Bob.

'I suppose they'll be my ancestors,' Jane said dubiously.

'What a bunch. I bet they were lads in their day. Doubtless they thought nothing of tickling Henry the Eighth on his favourite wife! Seemed to run to whiskers a lot, didn't they?'

Jane nodded absently. She was gazing at a face in the gloom — a face that sprouted a goodish deal of fungus about the chin and jowls.

Following her gaze, Bob laughed. 'That one looks almost real,' he said. 'Real enough to have a nest of birds in his whiskers ... *Hell!*' The last was wrung from him as the face they had been studying suddenly moved forward.

On closer examination, they observed that it was not, as they had assumed, another of the portraits, but was actually a thing of flesh and blood, framed in the entrance to a room.

'There are no *bird nests* in my beard, young man!' it observed acidly. Then: 'I take it you are Jane? I haven't had the pleasure of meeting you previously. I am Sir Mortimer Rivers, your father's brother.'

Jane stepped forward with a smile, extending her hand. 'This is a friend of mine, Mister ... *oh!*'

'Bob Carter's the name,' said Bob, stepping into the breach. 'Pleased to meet you, Sir Mortimer.'

'Hmm,' said that crusty individual. 'I'm afraid I can't say the same about you, young man! I find your remarks about my facial growth extremely impertinent.'

'Sorry about that,' Bob apologised. 'I thought you were another of those old butters up there, sir. Had no idea you were alive.'

'*Harrumph!*' snorted Sir Mortimer.

'Shall we adjourn into the library here, my dear? The rest of the family is already there, waiting for you.'

'Where's Mr. Stimson, the solicitor?' enquired Jane.

'Not here. We had a telephone call from him to say he would be rather late getting down to Riverton, and that if he was unable to get a taxi he wouldn't be arriving until tomorrow — in view of the Rivers' curse concerning strangers,' finished Sir Mortimer, eyeing Bob meaningfully.

'Well,' said Bob, grinning feebly, 'now you're among your relatives, Jane, I rather fancy I'll phone for a breakdown wagon and get back to the village.'

'I'm afraid that will be impossible,' grunted Sir Mortimer. 'The phone is out of order, young man.'

'But you said you had a phone call from the lawyer?' retorted Jane.

'We did — about an hour ago. But when I tried to make a call to the station to see if you had arrived, I failed to get through. I think that perhaps the storm has blown down the wires somewhere.'

There was nothing else for it. In spite of his disbelief in family curses and sinister butlers and all the rest of the stage drama paraphernalia, it was with a sinking heart that Bob Carter followed Jane and her uncle into the library.

Here they were introduced to two other members of the family. One was a hawk-faced woman, sharp of tongue and vinegary of aspect, attired in a rusty black gown, a pair of pince-nez and a stern expression. This was Esmeralda, the late Lucille Rivers' only sister. The other member was a vacuous, insipid-looking young man whose conversation seemed rather limited in the area of intelligent contributions. This specimen turned out to be Jane's other cousin. That was all that was left of the Rivers family.

3

Sudden Death!

It was a gloomy party that sat down to a cold supper served by Ashville. Conversation languished, and little was said until the supper things had been cleared away and they were seated round a dying fire, drinking glasses of an ancient vintage which Bob, with Jane's aid, had dug up in the old cellars.

'Funny thing,' mused Bob eventually, 'we heard a dog howling when we were on the way here. Came from the house, I think.'

'Dog!' exploded Sir Mortimer.

'By Gad!' said Archibald Rivers, the vacuous one.

'There is no dog for miles,' stated Esmeralda primly.

'That's queer,' Jane contributed. 'Could have sworn we heard one somewhere about here.'

'There are a lot of strange things about this house, my dear.' Sir Mortimer lit up a foul-smelling pipe and peered at them through the haze of smoke that rose from it. 'Let's face it — after all, Lucille was a funny woman. A very funny woman! I might almost say that she was mentally unhinged. That is why none of us ever visited her. Rivers End was never a comfortable place to stay. It is less so now. The manner of Lucille's death was strange, also. Mutilated beyond recognition, they say, as if by some wild beast! They found her in this very room, by the fireplace.'

'Absolutely!' agreed Archie wisely.

'I hardly think it is good-mannered to discuss intimate family affairs with a perfect stranger, Mortimer,' remarked Esmeralda acidly.

'Don't mind me,' put in Bob. 'I love a bit of cheery after-dinner talk, you know.'

Conversation died away again. Eventually Sir Mortimer yawned heavily and stretched his arms. 'I don't think Mr. Stimson will be here tonight after all,' he commented. 'So I, for one, suggest that we all retire. No point in hanging about waiting for the man if he isn't coming, is there?'

Archie, rising from his chair, nodded his assent cheerfully.

Ashville appeared as if by magic. 'I will conduct you to your rooms,' he leered.

'Not us, you won't, old bean,' Bob told him. 'Jane and I will sit up a bit longer.'

General good-nights were said, and then Sir Mortimer, Archie and Esmeralda were escorted up the staircase by Ashville.

'You know,' Bob said thoughtfully when they had gone, 'I don't like that bloke, Ashville. There's something decidedly smelly about him, if you ask me!'

'I think it's his socks,' said Jane, nodding.

'I see what you mean,' agreed Bob, 'but I didn't intend it so literally. I just meant that I don't like his face or his movements. The blessed chap's always leering, and coming into doorways that you fancied weren't there before. I mean, look at the way he sprang into being when Morty suggested going to roost! Almost as if he had been listening to us talking.'

'You're right,' agreed Jane. 'In fact, there's something very fishy about the whole business to me. I'm — I'm frightened, Bob.' She moved closer to him, and he wound a comforting arm about her shoulders.

'You must be tired,' he said. 'Hadn't you better be getting to bed?'

'Ooh, no! I think I'll sit up all night here. I feel so much safer when you're with me.'

'That's more than I do, honey,' Bob said, glancing apprehensively about. 'It's a funny thing that the telephone should fail at a time like this — very funny. Makes me think there may be some monkey business afoot.'

'We're letting our imaginations run away with us,' said Jane, smiling suddenly. 'It's because of all that gruesome talk at supper. We've been brooding on it too much, Bob. Still, I'm awfully glad I met you . . . I'd never have been able to stick it here all alone.'

'Wouldn't you?'

Her lips were very close, and very irresistible; at least, Bob found them so. Before he knew quite what he was doing, he had pulled her slender figure towards him and was pressing his mouth to hers. Jane raised no objection: in fact, she actually enjoyed it, and returned his embrace.

'Whew!' panted Bob, breaking away. 'You're certainly dynamite. I'm beginning to be glad I met you — in spite of what you've got me into!'

Jane smiled up at him, and as the firelight died away, she sank into a doze in his arms.

Left awake by himself, Bob began to notice weird cracking noises and stirrings in the big house. *What*, he thought, *am I doing here? What the hell have I let myself in for? Maybe I'd better scram while I'm still able. Jane'll be all right — this damned curse, or whatever it is, only applies to strangers. Yeah, maybe I'd better start hopping for home right now.*

Slowly he eased Jane on to the settee, glanced at her calm and lovely face as she slept serenely, and started to creep towards the library door.

Wait a minute, said his conscience sharply. *Where d'you think you're going, Bob Carter?*

To hell out of here! replied Bob's inner man.

Oh, are you! sneered his conscience. *So you're going to sneak out on that poor woman. My, my, I'm ashamed of you, Bob. Coward, that's what you are!*

Forget it, said the inner man. *That woman's nothing to me. Why should I risk my neck for her? What do I get for it?*

Who knows? his conscience said mysteriously. *After all, she's a very pretty woman, Bob. Isn't she, now? Just look at that golden hair, those promising lips ... She felt safe with you, didn't she? You wouldn't like her to think you're a yellow fool, would you?*

No, admitted the inner man reluctantly.

Go on, then! hissed his better half. *Go back there and take her in your arms, Bob!*

As he stood poised in indecision, Jane suddenly woke, gazed fearfully round her, and gave vent to a scarcely audible sob. 'Bob! Bob! Oh, where are you?'

'Here, honey,' Bob said, coming towards her. She wound her soft arms about his neck and pulled his face down to hers.

'Where were you, Bob? I sensed that you'd gone. I got so scared.'

'I — er — just went for a drink of water,' he lied calmly, and patted her shoulders comfortingly.

As they sat there listening to the creaking of the woodwork and the rumbling of thunder from outside, another sound broke into the stillness. *Thump! Thump! Thump!* It was the sound of measured footsteps on the floor above them. Bob could hear Jane inhale sharply.

The steps ceased as suddenly as they had begun. They listened in intent silence for several minutes, but the footsteps had ceased altogether.

'All right now,' whispered Bob. 'It was probably one of the others going for a — er — drink, or something.'

The words had scarcely left his lips when the screams began.

They began on a low gurgling note, rising in intensity until they were a series of high-pitched falsetto shrieks, torn from the throat of a person in indescribable torment. Shrilly they echoed through the silence of Rivers End, defying and drowning the noise of the thunder outside; volleying through the high oak-panelled halls and echoing down the long gloomy corridors.

Scream after scream rent the air; it was hard to believe that they could have come from any human throat. Then slowly they died away, ending in a blubbering, throaty cry. And as they did so another voice was raised in weird, maniacal laughter. For almost a minute the unearthly, unnatural mirth continued, then suddenly died away again. Once more the dullish clump of footsteps echoed above their heads, then all was still.

'What was *that*?' quavered Jane.

'I d-don't know,' mumbled Bob, heartily wishing he had never seen Rivers End.

'Where are the others? Surely they heard it?'

'If they've any sense,' said Bob, 'they're doing the same as we are — lying low and saying nothing.'

'Listen!' Jane gasped.

From the hall came the sound of heavy, dragging footsteps descending the stairs. Dragging down the steps uncertainly, as if the one who made them were blind.

Bob picked up the poker from the fireplace and held tightly to Jane's shoulders. 'Whatever it is, I'll rush it!' he said. 'You try to get out past it into the hall — then get away from this damned house!' He clenched his teeth, gripped the poker more tightly.

The steps were now dragging along the hall, heading directly for the door of the library. There was a clumsy fumbling at the handle of the door, then slowly it turned — the door began to swing open . . .

'Oh, Bob!' whispered Jane faintly.

A figure staggered through the door, advanced a pace towards them, stumbled, and flopped down just inside the room. It was the figure of Sir Mortimer Rivers. His features and his throat and pajamaed chest had been savagely ripped and slashed as if by some manner of wild beast.

Jane gave a shocked cry, then turned away from the body and buried her face in her hands. Bob gathered his remaining shreds of courage and crossed the room towards the mutilated figure.

'Poor devil's dead!' he exclaimed, rising from his examination. 'Jugular's severed!'

A light flashed on in the hall and Ashville, clad in dressing gown and carrying a lit candle, appeared. 'What is happening here ...' he began irately; then, his glance falling on the body: 'Sir Mortimer! How did this happen?'

'He's dead!' Bob said soberly. He covered the dead man's bloodstained beard and features with a fold of the dressing gown he was wearing.

'I heard screams,' said Ashville, 'and laughter.'

'So did we,' Bob told him tersely. Esmeralda and young Archibald had now entered the room and were gazing wide-eyed at the corpse on the floor.

'Where was everybody when this happened?' queried Bob.

'I was in my room,' said Esmeralda. 'I was too afraid to see what was wrong immediately.'

'I was asleep,' Archie contributed. 'Absolutely! Aunt Esme came in and woke me up to tell me about the screaming.'

'I was also in my room, sir. But I was cautious ...' said Ashville.

4

The Mystery Thickens

'Not working!' exclaimed Bob, clapping back the receiver on its rest. 'Sir Mortimer said it wasn't.'

'Then how on earth are we going to get in touch with the police?' asked Esmeralda fearfully.

They had covered the mutilated body of Sir Mortimer Rivers with his raincoat from the hall, and were now seated shivering round the dead fire in the library.

Ashville, slipping out of his role as butler, was seated with them, a worried frown on his usually evil features.

'What I don't understand,' said Bob thoughtfully, 'is how the other murder case wound up. I mean, what did the police do? Had they any idea who the killer was?'

All eyes were turned towards Ashville, who glanced down guiltily at his toes.

'Where were you when the old lady was murdered?' asked Bob.

'I was in London, sir. Miss Rivers sent me up there to get some articles she had ordered by phone. I was there the best part of the day — from twelve noon to about six o'clock in the evening. When I returned, the front door was open and I found Miss Rivers in here before the fire, horribly lacerated and torn!'

'Was there anyone else in the house?'

'No, sir. My wife should have been here, but she had vanished. I left her preparing lunch — my wife and I were the only servants the late Miss Rivers employed — and I haven't seen her since.'

'So when you returned, Miss Rivers was dead and your wife was missing? I don't want to jump to conclusions, Ashville, but doesn't that sound rather significant?'

Ashville nodded miserably. 'The police thought so, sir. They are even now searching for my wife to charge her with murder. But I wouldn't believe it of her, sir! Martha was a good woman — I should know, as we've been married for twenty years now. But what made things look more suspicious was the fact that all the money there had been in the house was also missing.'

'Do you think your wife might have returned? Is it possible that she is responsible for — that?' Bob indicated the covered corpse.

Ashville shook his head vehemently. 'No, sir! Definitely not! What possible purpose could Martha have for wishing to kill this man?'

Bob shook his head slowly. 'If we knew what purpose anyone could have for killing Sir Mortimer, we'd have as good as solved the mystery.'

'But how about the police?' chimed in Archie brightly. 'I mean, we can't very well leave dashed corpses cluttering up the jolly old ancestral home, can we?'

Ashville coughed deprecatingly. 'If it's agreeable to all of you, I'll go for the police. This house is getting on my nerves. I would welcome the opportunity of getting away from it for a time.'

'That all right by everybody?' asked Bob.

'No!' snapped Esmeralda. 'It is not! I intend to return to the village at once!'

'I hardly think that would do,' said Bob,

smiling. 'The police will wish us to remain here until they arrive.'

'Furthermore, madam,' elaborated Ashville, 'the road to the village is somewhat dangerous for a lady of your years.'

'I beg your pardon?' barked Esmeralda frostily. 'What do you mean, my good man, by 'a lady of my years'?'

'Nothing, madam. I merely meant for a lady in her prime.'

'Oh, I see,' said Esmeralda, somewhat mollified. 'But I could accompany you, Ashville. You could show me the way.'

'Very well, madam! I will bring your coat and hat.' Ashville left the room reluctantly.

'I don't like that man,' burbled Archie as the butler vanished. 'I smell something jolly niffy about him.'

'That's exactly what I said,' said Bob, nodding. 'It's quite on the cards that he's the murderer ...'

'... and *doesn't* intend to go for the police at all!' concluded Jane.

'Suppose he's in some deep game with his wife!'

A sudden gulp made them glance towards Esmeralda. Her face had gone strangely pale and her knees were dithering. 'Er — you — you think that Ashville might be the murderer?' she stammered weakly.

'Quite likely, I should say,' replied Bob.

'Good heavens!' she gasped, horrified. 'And I might have gone out with him into the darkness.'

The door opened and Ashville re-entered, bearing Esmeralda's coat and hat and wearing his own rainproof mackintosh, buttoned up to the chin.

'Hem — er — on — er — second thought, Ashville,' stuttered Esmeralda, 'I don't think I'll venture out in this weather. I — er — I'm not very agile now, you know.'

Ashville looked relieved. 'As you wish, madam. I will return as speedily as possible with the police.'

They sat looking at each other as the front door closed after him with a hollow, echoing sound. Then suddenly, Jane started to her feet.

'What's that?' said Archie.

'A howling sound — almost a screaming!' said Bob.

They listened intently.

'The wind,' sighed Bob after several

tense minutes. 'It's been screeching like that for the last three hours. We're just letting our nerves get the better of us.'

'Sounds almost human to me,' Jane whispered. 'Just like that howling we heard on our way up here!'

Esmeralda, tight-lipped, stood up. 'I'm going to my room,' she told them. 'If one of you gentlemen would be kind enough to see me up the stairs …?'

'Don't be silly,' said Jane. 'You'd better stay here with us!'

'No thank you! I shall feel much safer behind a locked and bolted door.'

Simultaneously the others rose.

'Very well,' agreed Bob. 'We'll all see you safely to your cubbyhole. Come on!'

Glancing fearfully at each shadow, they started up the wide, shadowy staircase, then turned down the passage at the top.

'Is this it?' Bob indicated an open door on the right.

'Er — yes. I wonder if you'd mind looking under the bed and in the wardrobe for me?'

Bob grinned in spite of himself and did as asked. 'All clear,' he announced, rising.

Esmeralda turned round in the doorway. 'Young man,' she said, addressing Bob, 'I should feel much easier in my mind if you promised to be within calling distance.'

'Don't worry — if you get lonely, just shout. We'll be able to hear you from the library.'

The door closed and the key turned in the lock.

'I don't think she'll be so safe there,' mused Jane. 'But still, what can we do? Can't very well squat up here outside her door all night.'

'Absolutely not!' agreed Archie, and they returned to the library.

For a time they talked of anything to relieve the strain on their nerves. Then Archie's mouth opened, his head fell back on the chair, and a refined snore issued from his lips.

'Hark!' chuckled Bob. 'The plaintive note of a sleeping man about town.'

Jane smiled tremulously and snuggled up closer to him. They relaxed on the settee, half dozing.

Bob became aware of the thing outside the window first. The long French windows were not curtained or shuttered, and with each brilliant sheet of lightning that flashed across the stormy heavens, the exterior of the house and window was revealed clearly. It was during one of these flashes that, gazing sleepily at the window, Bob became conscious of a ghastly white figure glaring in. Rain had so blurred the panes that it was impossible to say exactly what it was, and by the time Bob had gained his feet and rushed across there was nothing visible except the garden.

'Bob!' panted Jane, suddenly coming to full wakefulness. 'What is it?'

'Nothing, Jane. I simply imagined I saw someone peering in at us.' He tried to open the windows without success. 'Jammed!' he grated. 'I'm going round to the front door, Jane, to have a quick look round.' He picked up the poker again.

'I'm coming with you!' Jane said determinedly.

'All right — if you want to. I think Archibald will be quite safe there for a few minutes.'

Leaving the sleeping, snoring Archie in the chair, they emerged into the hall and tiptoed towards the front door. Cautiously Bob turned the handle and began to ease it open. Then the wind, forcing itself against the opening door, flung it violently inwards together with the body of a man in a raincoat!

'Ashville!' screamed Jane, her nerves snapping.

Ashville was, without a doubt, dead. His face and body were ripped and maltreated as Sir Mortimer's had been, and he was a sickly sight to look upon.

'He mustn't have got any further than the doorstep,' said Bob soberly. 'Perhaps the screaming we thought was the wind was really Ashville … It seems almost as though he were killed to prevent him going for the police!' He grasped the door, and by exerting all his energy managed to shut it again. 'Poor old Ashville,' he said in a low voice. 'How we misjudged the poor chap. Holy smoke! It might have been me lying there if he hadn't volunteered to go!' He gulped loudly.

'What are we going to do with him?' Jane held tight to his arm, white-faced.

'I'm afraid we'll have to leave him where

he is. What's more, it's no use anyone else going for the police. Probably they'd only get the same as Ashville. We can only wait until morning and go for them then — if there's any of us left alive to go!'

'Oh, Bob, don't talk that way, please!'

'Sorry,' Bob told her. 'I've got a misplaced sense of humour, I guess. But I really do think ... *hell!*'

He was cut off short, for as he spoke, from the top floor came a series of terror-stricken shrieks, shrilling through the silent house.

'Esmeralda!' gasped Bob. Then, although he was scared silly, he took the stairs two at a time, with Jane close behind him.

5

So Long, Archie

When they arrived at the door to Esmeralda's room, the horror-stricken shrieks were still ringing out. They could now distinguish words, with cries for help mingled with them.

'Mr. Carter ... help ... oh, oh, *oh*!'

'Open up, if you can!' yelled Bob, rattling the closed door.

There was a flurried movement inside the room and a scraping of key in lock. Then the door flew open and Esmeralda rushed out.

'In the wardrobe,' she gasped weakly. 'Something — something *alive* ... moving. I was trying to get to sleep when I heard it scrabbling at the wardrobe door ... I was too scared to move till you came ...'

Bob gripped the poker and peered in. He looked dubiously at the ancient oak wardrobe that was built in to the wall.

‘Hmm,’ he said thoughtfully.

‘Well?’ demanded Esmeralda, having recovered from her fright. ‘Aren’t you going to see what’s inside it?’

Er — ah — hem …’ spluttered Bob, stealing a glance at Jane.

She was looking at him expectantly. Obviously she was relying on him. Bob was sorrier than ever that he’d got into all this.

‘There it is again,’ gasped Esmeralda. ‘Go and see what it is, young man, in that wardrobe!’

‘In — er — the — er — wardrobe,’ hedged Bob.

‘I said the wardrobe, young man!’

‘That’s what I thought you said, the — er — wardrobe. But on second thought, perhaps it would be safer if we didn’t pry too closely — I mean, with you ladies being here, I don’t know if I’ve the right to open that door and put you in danger. If there were only myself to think of …’

‘We don’t mind,’ said Jane quickly. ‘See what it is, Bob. We’d better make an effort to find something out.’

‘But suppose there *is* something dangerous in there?’ Bob said. ‘What if it leaps out and floors me? How about you two?'

'That will be all right, young man,' said Esmeralda primly. 'I have the door key here, and we can shut and lock this door to it, whatever it is.'

'Leaving me on the inside?'

'Certainly! I hope that in the circumstances, you wouldn't expect two women to dash in to your rescue, Mr. Carter?'

'Huh!' Bob stepped into the room and over to the wardrobe, his knees beating a tattoo. The key was already in the lock. Holding his breath and his poker, he turned it, gave the door a slight push, and jumped back.

He was in time to see a dark shape vanishing through a panel at the rear of the large wardrobe. A peal of insane, harsh laughter floated back to their ears when the panel finally closed, shutting them off from the secret passage behind it.

Jane and Esmeralda, standing in the doorway ready to bolt, had not seen the passage, and Bob thought it best not to upset them by mentioning it. He turned round, composing his features and spreading his arms helplessly. 'Nothing here,' he told them.

'What was that — that horrible laughter?' Jane enquired.

'Laughter? Oh, of course. Well, it seemed to come from the back of this wall.'

'Are you sure there's nothing there?' Esmeralda gulped. 'Look again, young man. There *must* be something!'

'But there isn't,' Bob told them. He stepped inside the wardrobe, and they entered the room and peered in after him. He lit a cigarette and took a deep drag from it, then leaned nonchalantly against the back paneling. That was where he made his big mistake! Through some odd chance, his elbow touched the spot that operated the mechanism of the panel. Before the shocked gaze of the two women, it opened, and Bob shot backwards into darkness ungracefully. Then the panel closed again between himself and the ladies.

'Oh, Bob!' screamed Jane. 'Bob, come back!'

From beyond the thick woodwork came

a muffled voice: 'Hey! Get me out of this!'

'How ... how?' Jane began to frantically run her hands over various projections in the wardrobe, without success. 'Oh, Bob, I can't find the thing that works it!' she exclaimed tremulously.

'Damn!' came his voice. 'It's pitch black in here. It's a sort of passage or something. Listen — I've still got this poker. I'm going to follow it along a bit. If you don't hear from me within about half an hour, call the nearest undertaker — if you can find the body!'

They heard his muffled footsteps receding, then they turned to each other silently, with a wild surmise ...

Then the nerve-wracking screams started again!

They echoed up from below this time, and the two women clung to each other in silent terror. The screams ran on and on for what seemed to them ages; then they broke off. And following abruptly in the accentuated silence came that peal of shrill, maniacal cackling, making them twitch with nerves and causing their blood to turn to water in their veins.

'Archie!' babbled Jane as silence fell again. 'I'm going down to see — to see what's happened to him.'

The older woman clung to her with desperate, claw-like fingers. 'You can't!' she sobbed wildly. 'You'll be killed. You can't leave me here alone!'

'Let go of me,' hissed Jane. 'I'm not going to stay here when someone's being murdered — when I might be able to help to save him.' Breathlessly, controlling her panic with an effort, she tore away from Esmeralda's grasp and ran along the corridor, down the stairs, and into the library.

Archie, whom they had left peacefully snoring, was stretched out on the same chair. His face and body were ripped and slashed in the same way as the others.

Jane paused, her breath ripping harshly from her strained throat. Esmeralda had followed her down and was standing behind her, sobbing with fear. 'Is he dead?' the older woman asked.

Jane pushed aside her horror and walked round the pool of blood on the floor, to a spot behind the chair where she could examine Archie. He was dead all right. As with the others who had been murdered — slaughtered would be a better word — the slashes on his body were clean, neat cuts; the flesh was parted almost to the bone, and the jugular vein was completely severed.

'Oh, dear! I do wish Mr. Carter were here!' quavered Esmeralda, and Jane found herself in hearty agreement with her.

'Poor Archie,' she whispered. 'How could anyone want to harm him? He was such an inoffensive sort of chap.'

'There's a fiend in this house!' stormed Esmeralda. 'We'll all be murdered — I feel it in my bones. Horrible, horrible!'

From outside, battering against the windows, the thunder and the wind seemed to echo her statement.

'Look!' cried Jane, pointing to the panelled wall near the fireplace.

Esmeralda looked and beheld a gaping dark hole, some three feet across and five feet high. Beyond this aperture, all was darkness. Even as they watched, slow, slithering steps became audible in the passage.

Petrified, they crouched back against the wall, unable to speak or move. Then, as the footsteps grew louder and nearer, Jane recovered, snatched up a pair of fire tongs, and concealed herself behind the swinging pane.

A dark figure suddenly stepped into the room, bearing a weapon in its right hand. Closing her eyes and breathing a prayer, Jane smashed the fire tongs down on its head with all her might!

Thud. The prowler was down.

'It's a man!' said Jane, kneeling beside the figure. She extended a tentative hand and rolled him onto his back so that the face was in view.

'*Bob!*' she shrieked.

'*Mr. Carter!*' screeched Esmeralda.

'Bob, Bob, dear,' moaned Jane, cradling his head on her lap. 'Oh, what have I done? I've killed him! Oh, Bob, I'm sorry . . . Speak to me, Bob . . . Bob, *speak to me!*'

Bob's eyes flickered open. He felt his head with an exploratory hand.

'Speak to me, Bob — say you're all right, dear!' pleaded Jane.

'Anybody get the number of the truck

that hit me?' said Bob feebly.

'I hit you, dear,' cried Jane. 'I thought you were someone else!'

'I wish I was. My coconut feels as if it's been used for a battering ram! What did you hit me with, the fender?'

'No, dear. Only the fire tongs.'

'What's *that*?' Bob gave a convulsive jump.

'That's poor Archie. He's been murdered.'

'Now I've got it! I went down the secret passage in the wardrobe, didn't I? And it led down some steps. Then I heard a whole lot of screaming going on. That would be Archie. And I was just emerging cautiously into this room when you hit me with the fire tongs.' He hauled himself to his feet and allowed Jane to inspect his aching skull.

'No breaks,' she announced with relief.

'That's surprising,' said Bob gloomily. 'It feels as if it's been driven down to the region of my fifth waistcoat button! You've a pretty hefty slosh, honey.'

'I know. I play golf.'

'You do? That accounts for it, then.

And I thought you were a weak, tender woman. Ye gods! I suppose if ever you get married you'll chivvy your husband about with the business end of a mashie niblick.'

Soberly, Bob draped a tablecloth over the body of Archie. Although his words were light, his expression was grim. He knew that it depended on him to keep up the morale of the three of them. Another murder like this and there was a chance of the women being permanently affected. Lesser things have unhinged the human mind before today.

'I do wish Ashville would hurry back with the police,' said Esmeralda fretfully. Jane glanced at Bob, and Bob realised that the older woman was as yet unaware of Ashville's demise.

'Ashville won't be coming back,' he said slowly. 'He isn't in the land of the living anymore.'

'No! No! Surely nothing has — nothing has happened to — to Ashville?' quivered Esmeralda.

'I'm afraid so. Now take it easy! He was killed before he'd hardly left the house.'

'*Ack!*' yelped Esmeralda, and flopped on to the settee in a fit of hysterics.

Jane rallied round and patted her hands while Bob waited patiently for her screeching to cease. When Esmerelda had more or less regained her composure, he faced both women and spoke sharply.

'We stick together for the rest of the night,' he rapped. 'It's our only chance! I don't know what reason there could be for all these murders, but they seem to be the work of a maniac. So we'll stick to this room and chance it. I'd advise you both to have some kind of weapon handy, just in case.'

Eventually, when they were armed with tongs, poker and shovel, Bob arranged three armchairs back to back so that, when occupied, they would command an all-round view of the library. Then they took positions and settled down as well as they could.

Half an hour later, by Bob's watch, footsteps started up above. *Thud, thud, thud* they went over the heads of the three nervous vigilantes. Then came the horrible laughter, rising higher, and higher and seeming to mock their puniness as they sat helplessly waiting for whatever might be in store. The laughter reached a crescendo, then died away again.

'Sit tight,' called Bob comfortingly. 'As long as we stay here, nobody can get in the room without being seen.'

They sat tight as the footsteps descended stairs. They sat tight as the laughter shrilled along the passage outside. And they sat tight as it issued from the very walls about them.

'Suppose — suppose we all take a chance and try to get to the village?' whispered Jane.

'I think it better to stay here,' Bob said. 'The creature, whatever it is, may just be waiting for us to get outside. Look how easily it got Ashville once he left the house! Besides, none of us know the way to the village, and it's dangerous country in these parts.'

They sat on in silence. Unexpectedly, the electric light blinked out.

'Matches!' cried Bob. 'Have you any, Jane?'

'I thought you had!' she exclaimed.

'I must have dropped them when I lit that cigarette in the wardrobe! Have you any, Miss Rivers?'

'N-n-no!'

'Then sit where you are — and if anything comes near you, hit out!'

So they sat in the darkness, listening in terror to the slithering footsteps that were coming nearer … nearer …

6

Blind Man's Bluff

It was over within five minutes.

They sat in silence until a sudden movement from Esmeralda's chair heralded the advent of the prowler.

'It's here!' she shrilled in panic. 'It's right by my chair! I can feel it touching me!'

'Hit out!' yelled Bob, leaping to his feet. There was the sound of a heavy blow, and a yelp of animal-like fury, and then Esmeralda commenced screaming. Jane started up in helpless horror.

'The lights, Jane, try the lights!' shouted Bob, hurling himself round the chairs towards Esmeralda. His clutching fingers sought in the darkness: sought, and found a hold on the clothing of a bony body. A musty, unclean stench almost caused him to vomit, but he held on and struck out savagely with the poker. His arm was seized in an amazingly strong grip, and a set of steel talons raked down his unprotected features.

'Blast you!' he roared, pain and agony robbing him of his fright. Again and again he lashed out with his weapon, hearing the blows strike home on a soft surface. A succession of grunts escaped the murderer, then a hard blow smashed into Bob's stomach, and his clutch weakened and fell away. 'Lights!' he yelled again.

'They — they aren't working,' sobbed Jane.

They stood in the black stillness and listened. There was a creak of woodwork, as if a panel had opened and shut again.

'It's gone, whatever it was,' breathed Bob.

'What — what happened?' whimpered Jane.

Bob made no reply. It had just occurred to him that the corpse of Archie might have matches in its pocket. Distastefully, he fumbled through the jacket and was rewarded by a box of Swan Vestas. He struck one.

The feeble glow revealed a scene of carnal destruction.

Esmeralda lay on the floor. She had been more savagely slashed than any of the others, and the jugular vein was hanging from her almost severed neck in a crimson, gory mess, together with her torn windpipe and ligaments. She was dead, of course.

Bob himself had five lateral gashes running down his right cheek, which were streaming blood. Only by a miracle had the thing missed his eye.

'Bob!' cried Jane as she beheld the dreadful state he was in.

'It's all right — just superficial,' he said reassuringly. 'Main thing is to get hold of some light. How about Ashville? If he had intended to go to the village, he would have taken a torch with him. And that being so, it's ten to one it's still in his pocket.'

He was right, for when they searched the dead butler's rainproof coat they found a bull's eye torch in the pocket.

'Come on,' Jane said. 'We'll have to find the kitchen and fix your face.'

Together they crept along the hall. The kitchen wasn't so hard to find — it led off a short passage at the rear. Here, in the glow of the torch, Jane tenderly washed

Bob's wounds and tore strips from her underskirt to bind them with. 'How can I stop them bleeding?' she asked worriedly.

'Just a second.' Bob stood up and, crossing to a cupboard, opened it. On the top shelf he found a bag of salt. He poured this onto the narrow table, then pressed his torn cheek into it.

The agony was almost unbearable, but he endured it until the salt had become thickly caked on his cheek. Then Jane wrapped the torn strips of underskirt round his head, longways, to hold the salt in position.

When she had finished, Bob presented rather a ludicrous appearance. He resembled a man suffering from a severe gumboil, or a prize case of the mumps. He peered in a mirror and couldn't restrain a grin.

'The hero gets his,' he chuckled. 'Ouch! I bet you didn't think when I met you that before the night was out, I'd be wearing a portion of one of your more intimate garments round my countenance! You've practically swathed me like a mummy, honey! I feel like the Invisible Man, or a relic from the Battle of Bannockburn. Suppose I get another raking — what the dickens will you use for bandages next time?'

'Next time,' Jane replied sternly, 'I'll use a piece of this rough toweling here. See? So you can stop gloating right now, Bob Carter!'

Bob drew her to him and kissed her. Jane's arms stole round his neck, and for a moment they forgot the terrors still in store for them.

'Honey,' Bob said, some five minutes later, 'I've got an idea! It's a pip; but you'll have to be brave about it.'

'Go on, Bob,' she said.

'Well, in the first place it seems as though the lights have been cut off at the mains box. Now we can't very well go rooting about for that in a house this size — it could be anywhere! So there's only one thing left to do; you'll need all your nerve for it, darling.

'This is the idea. Whatever this murderous thing is, it seems to have a fair idea of our movements. Probably it's spying on us from these secret passages.' His voice sank to a hushed whisper. 'But if you creep back to the library, using Archie's matches to find the way, and I sneak after you with the torch, maybe we can work the trick. Make as much noise as you can on the way back, and keep striking matches. I'll stick to the torch and shimmy along behind you, making no noise at all.

'When you get to the library, sit down in the chair and strike a few of Archie's matches to let it know you're there — if it's watching. Then wait in the darkness. Meanwhile, I'll have sneaked in and hidden behind the chair. When the damned thing starts creeping up on you, I'll be ready with the poker and the torch, and we'll finish things off one way or another. How about it, Jane?'

'Just as you say, Bob. It'll be better than hanging around not knowing what to do.'

'You're a heroine.' Bob smiled. He kissed her again; then, handing her the matches, he switched off the torch.

Jane moved along to the library, striking plenty of matches as she went. Behind her, some ten feet in the rear and out of the match light, crept Bob.

The first part of the plan ran smoothly. Jane gained the chair and sat down. Bob sneaked in behind her and crouched low behind the chair back. Neither of them spoke.

Almost before they were in position, the mad laughter began again. In the chair, Jane shuddered; and behind it, Bob tensed.

Then the footsteps — slow, slithering footsteps — approached the chair. Jane could stand it no longer.

'Bob!' she shrieked. 'The torch ...' And springing up, Bob switched the torch on.

7

Fiend at Her Heels!

Outlined in the beam of light was a figure so repulsively horrible that Bob almost dropped the torch. It stood not three feet from Jane, blinking owlishly in the sudden glare. In its right hand — which was raised, ready to strike — was a peculiar pad on which five sharp blades glittered evilly.

It was the murderer — or rather, the murderess; for it was a woman!

Gaunt and unkempt-looking, with filthy wisps of grey hair protruding from beneath the edges of a soiled bonnet such as was worn in Victoria's day, her mottled, filthy features and thin lips were drawn back in an insane snarl from rotted, uneven teeth. The picture was completed by the madness that glared from the yellowish eyes. All of which presented a strange contrast to the dingy black dress that covered the bent body.

Only for a moment did the creature pause. Then her arm began to descend towards Jane's pale face, the cruel knives sparkling with the reflection of the torchlight.

But before those knives could strike, Bob had thrown the poker with unerring accuracy; and as he did so, he pulled the chair violently backwards, hurling Jane to the floor.

It was only this quick movement that saved Jane life-long disfigurement, if not death! For in spite of the impact of the poker on her face, the madwoman continued her downward slice, and Jane shot backwards just as the blades approached her features.

Rapidly, Bob sprang forward and grasped the poker once more. And when the madwoman came at him, shrieking insanely, he was forced to strike out at her mercilessly. The knob of the iron poker crashed into her eyes again and again until, with a stricken moan, she dropped the weapon she carried and scurried away into the shadows, vanishing through an open panel in the wall.

'You all right, Jane?' said Bob, helping the dazed woman to her feet.

'Yes, thanks to you, Bob! What a horrible old woman! Is she Ashville's wife?'

'I expect so! I rather think we've hurt her badly. I had to hit her in the face or she'd have killed us both. Look, she hasn't closed the panel.'

Picking up the devilish murder instrument, Bob took Jane's hand, and they went through the panel into the tunnel beyond. There came to their ears the sound of anguished moaning — the pitiful cries of someone in unbearable agony.

'Must be terribly injured,' Bob said quietly. 'Come on, the noises are coming from round this corner!'

They turned the corner, the beam from Bob's torch shining revealingly ahead. They were in a smaller branch passage which led downwards into pitch blackness. The moans were fainter now, as if the madwoman had managed to put more distance between them.

'You can go back and wait in the library if you wish,' Bob said, glancing at the pale-faced woman.

'Oh, no, Bob! I wouldn't dare,' said Jane with a shudder. Bob took her hand comfortingly and they pressed on into the darkness.

The passage inclined steeply for about fifteen yards, then ended in a short flight of steps. They were damp and covered with green slime. The two descended and came to a halt in front of an immense bolt-studded door that was slightly ajar. As they listened tensely, from behind it issued the sound of unmistakable moaning.

'Stay here, Jane,' Bob told her tersely. 'She's dropped her original weapon, but heaven only knows what other horrible contrivances she may have!'

Jane nodded mutely. She had no wish to venture beyond that door. As long as Bob was between herself and the horrible old madwoman, she didn't feel so afraid.

Shining his torch straight ahead, Bob pushed open the door and went cautiously forward. He shone his torch carefully round the small chamber he was in, and was about to call out to Jane that the woman didn't seem to be there, when a stealthy movement behind him made him whirl about, poker raised.

He was too late. Even as he turned, something heavy crashed upon his head; and for the second time that night, Bob lurched to the floor, completely unconscious.

As he did so, the madwoman threw herself towards the door behind which Jane stood and slammed it shut, separating Jane from the chamber. Then she glanced down at the unconscious man before her, and crossed the room and left by yet another heavy door. This also she locked.

★ ★ ★

Jane was unaware that anything was wrong until the door had been slammed in her face. Neither Bob nor she had imagined that the madwoman would retain her cunning in spite of the terrible injuries she had received. Jane had merely seen a dark form leap from behind the half-closed door, holding a bar of some description; then, before she could warn Bob, the bar had fallen and the woman had turned and slammed the door on her.

The realisation that Bob was trapped in the chamber, most likely unconscious, and with the murderess, made her start to beat hysterically against the wooden beams. For what seemed to her hours she pounded away, screaming 'Bob!', but finally she had to desist from sheer weariness.

Sanity came back to her, and slowly and methodically she began the search for a button or lever that would open the impassable barrier. Surely there must be one somewhere — there had to be. But what was going on inside? If anything had happened to Bob, she felt she would go raving mad, alone in this house except for the murderess.

'Oh,' she breathed, 'please — please let him be alive and unhurt! Please let him answer me somehow!'

But though Jane stopped several times to listen at the door, there was no sound from within. When her search was finished, her nails and fingers were torn and bleeding from the coarse stones of the wall. She had found nothing that would re-open the sealed door.

Wearily she sank down on to the bottom step and began to sob pitifully. 'Oh, Bob ... Bob!' Tears trickled from her smarting eyes and down onto her thin dress. She wiped them away with the back of her hand, rose determinedly, and began the search again.

But it was hopeless. The bolt-studded door remained immovable before her, seeming to mock her feeble efforts. It had been built in the days when doors were made to stay put, unless one had the means of opening them.

Then a new idea struck her. Perhaps there was another entrance to the chamber! Perhaps, if she tried some of the side passages she had passed with Bob, she would discover a method of reaching the spot where he lay by means of a second doorway!

The thought stimulated her. For the moment, so worried was she about Bob that she had almost forgotten the madwoman might be still at large. She turned and began to retrace her movements: up the steps, and along the passage which led to the library.

Unexpectedly, in the dim light from one of the matches that she had retained, two narrow tunnels appeared in the darkness on either side of her. Her heart thumping madly, she chose the right-hand one. Falteringly, a sense of some unseen peril within her, she commenced to tread down the passage.

Abruptly she paused and stood stock-still. Someone was behind her; someone was following her down the passage, silently, craftily, waiting to spring at her and rend her with cruel talons!

Jane sensed this. She hadn't actually heard or seen anything, yet some extra sense warned her that she was in terrible danger.

She walked a few steps further. Stopped. This time she distinctly heard slithering steps halting suddenly. Quietly she extracted a match from the box, wishing she had had the foresight to bring one of the candles from the hall. The match scraped against the sandpaper and flared into life. As it did so, Jane whirled round, holding it before her.

The madwoman was standing almost on top of her, a short steel bar clutched in her gnarled hands! Blood was trickling in red rivulets down her battered features, dripping from the end of her witch-like chin. One eye was a horribly mangled mess, hanging down her left cheek, exuding yellowish slime. But the other was ablaze with a fierce, insane glare; a glare of hatred and bloodlust. From between the creature's fang-like teeth came a snarl of incredible fury — a snarl such as a wounded dog might make.

For a second neither moved. The flaring match painted the scene with a weird light, then slowly dimmed and died away.

Fear bubbled in Jane's breast, surged upwards to her palpitating heart, and tore from her lips in a horrified shriek. Then she was running blindly, madly, without regard for safety ... running into the unwholesome jaws of the black tunnel ... running from the look in that malignant eye ... And behind her, like some obscene ghoul from the grave, raced the murderess.

Bob was dismissed from Jane's mind now. Her only thought was to escape from the monstrosity that pursued her; to get out into the night, into the storm, and run and run until the cottages of Riverton appeared before her, and she could rush into the comfortable security of the village police station and stammer out her tale of dread to some kindly, stolid sergeant who would comfort and protect her.

In fancy she could feel the impact of the iron bar crushing her unprotected neck, smashing life from her tired body. She could feel the fetid breath of the fiend at her heels, and knew that her desperate race was hopeless; that even if she were to put up a struggle, she would stand no chance against a madwoman.

Down passage after passage she panted, in inky darkness; guessing, more by instinct than anything else, the twists and turns of the tunnel. Then suddenly, before she could stop herself, she cannoned headlong into a massive wooden beam, her forehead striking violently against it. Immediately her fears were blotted out, as without a sound she sank to the slimy floor.

8

Bob in a Jam!

Bob Carter groaned and ran a weak hand over the base of his skull. He was aware that he was lying on a damp floor somewhere, that his face was heavily bandaged, and that his head ached infernally.

Vague, unreal thoughts flitted across his dazed memory: images of a wild-eyed old woman with a fearsome weapon, and dimly formed pictures of a pretty, golden-haired woman.

But somehow they seemed far away, these things. Shadowy and unfocused. Vainly he tried to drag his erring memory back to the events that had led up to his present state, but his mind steadfastly refused to come to the scratch.

He pulled himself upright against the wall, and his bent knees made contact with something hard and round. He groped for it in the nothingness and found that it was a torch.

A torch! Somehow that seemed to bring back more vague memories — dark passages ... a bolt-studded door ... a small, dismal chamber — could that be what he was in now? But if so, how had he come here? And what else was missing from his mental pictures? He groaned again and shook his head to clear the fuzziness from his brain.

He seemed to recall a sinister kind of butler ... what was his name? There had been a lot of screaming, and the sound of thudding footsteps.

His mind was like a half-formed jigsaw puzzle, and try as he would he could not fit in the missing pieces.

He pressed the switch on the torch, and was relieved when a beam of light sprang from the end. Curiously, he directed it round the stone-walled room he was in. There were two doors, each of which he tried. Both were locked or fastened in some way.

He sat down again, placing the light beside him, then felt in his pocket for a cigarette and inserted it between his teeth.

No matches! Matches ...? Where did

they fit into the puzzle? Somewhere, he was sure. He seemed to remember that matches had been very important to him not so long ago.

What the devil was he doing in here? Who'd hit him across the head, and why? What was it all about?

The more he concentrated, the more his brain blurred over; and after some minutes he shrugged his shoulders and dismissed the matter from his mind. He could reason it all out at some future date. The immediate problem was to get out of this filthy hole.

He rose again and examined the walls carefully. Since the two doors boasted no keyholes, he assumed that they must operate by a mechanism of some description. A careful search failed to reveal anything that might open them, however. Maybe they opened from the outside?

Once more he went over the walls closely, then the doors. His attention was attracted by the iron studs that were set in the woodwork evenly, about three inches from each other. Patiently he went over them, pushing, pulling, and trying to twist them sideways. And on the top right-hand corner stud, he found what he was after. At his first push, the door gave a protesting creak and swung open!

Bob passed through it and found himself in a dark passage. He seemed to remember it, but not very clearly. He went along it rapidly, feeling that the sooner he found the way out of this hole he was in, the better. Two smaller passages branched off to his right and left, but these he ignored entirely, feeling that they could not lead him anywhere in particular. He followed the main tunnel; and sure enough, before long his torch shone on an open, square space, and he emerged into the library.

It was unfortunate that he failed to focus on the scene of destruction and death there. Had he done so, it was probable that everything would have been clear to him once again. But his torch found the door immediately; and without bothering to glance round, he went straight across the room and through the door. Down a long hall, facing him, was what he took to be the front entrance; and lying slightly to one side, dimly seen in the outermost radius of the torchlight, was a huddled heap.

This, if Bob had only taken the trouble to investigate, was Ashville. He didn't feel much like investigating, however. The bump on his head was throbbing painfully, and gaunt pangs of agony shot up and down the side of his lacerated face.

With an angry grunt, he tore open the front door and, leaving it swinging wide, put his head down and pushed on into the teeth of the black heavens.

The swaying treetops above him howled savage defiance at the vivid flashes of lightning. The rain, buffeted by the savage wind, lashed down on his bared head, quickly soaking him to the skin, and pasting his trousers to his legs. Beneath his feet, mud and fallen leaves squelched forbiddingly. Somehow he found the road and staggered out onto it. His thin jacket was wrenched about by the fury of the gale, and sudden gusts of wind hurled enormous raindrops into his already smarting eyes. The torn underskirt with which Jane had bandaged his cheek was pulled from his face by invisible hands and hurled into the face of the storm.

The roadway began to drop suddenly, and the torch revealed a nasty chasm yawning before him. Bob cursed, swung round, and retraced his steps until he found the irregular rutted track which served as a road. His shoes squelching at every stride, he plodded on. The sooner he reached civilisation and had his injuries attended to, the better. There would be time enough to inform the police about the apparently deserted house, and to find out just what had occurred there.

Something loomed up before him, and in a momentary flash of lightning he beheld a car by the roadside, almost half buried in a waterlogged ditch. He tried the door, and realised with a start that it was his own car! His own car, here, halfway up a mountainside, buried in a ditch, umpteen miles from nowhere!

He slid in the driver's seat and fumbled for the half-bottle of brandy he invariably kept in the side pocket. The liquor shot down his throat, warming him and sending new energy into his worn-out frame.

He tried to figure things out again, and rapidly the missing pieces of the jigsaw slid into position. The station — the woman — the lift to Rivers End — the butler — the murders — the secret passages — the chamber — the attack by the madwoman! It all fitted! The dazedness had gone, and the menial pictures formed quickly and clearly. But Jane ... Good God! Had he left her there, in that damned house, with the old madwoman? He must get back at once! How could he have been so blind as to almost forget all that had happened? He shuddered to think that but for the car and the brandy, he might have gone wandering dazedly on to the village.

Perhaps he was too late even now! The thought made him lurch from the car and start in a staggering run back to the house. Gluey slush clung desperately to his feet, while the wind and rain tried to force him back away from Rivers End. Doggedly he kept on, hardly heedful of the elements which conspired against him to bar his return. Along the road ... into the drive ... up the steps ... into the house. He had to be in time, he had to! If anything had happened to Jane, he swore grimly to himself that he would kill the madwoman with his own hands!

He tripped across Ashville's corpse and almost fell. He raced frantically into the library, towards the opening in the wall.

There was no opening!

In his muddled condition he had not even a clear idea of which panel had been the one he had passed through.

The breath rasped from his throat as he gazed desperately round. There was no time to start a methodical search for the mechanism of the secret panel. Surely there must be another way … Of course there was! The wardrobe in what had been Esmeralda's room! There was an entrance to the passage in that!

His feet barely met the floor as he tore from the library and up the stairs. Esmeralda's door was still open; so was the wardrobe. He almost fell in; then, remembering how he had found the entrance before, he turned and leaned backwards against the rear of the woodwork. It opened and precipitated him inwards. He picked himself up and hurried down the corridor, the torch cutting a thin path of light into the darkness.

Once again he found himself in the passage that ran parallel with the library. He reached the branch tunnels and paused a second in indecision. As he stood there, from the right-hand tunnel came a muffled cry.

Pausing only to get a tighter grip on the torch, he ran in the direction of the call.

9

Motive for Murder

When Jane regained her senses, after colliding with the crossbeam in the dark passage, she found herself securely bound up with rope. A glance about her served to show that she was in the wine cellars. On either side of her rose tiers of long-empty barrels and kegs, and she was lying with her back to a number of bins. Over to the right, a flight of stone steps led upwards, and she recognised these as the steps she had descended earlier with Bob when they had obtained the after-dinner bottle of wine.

A candelabra was placed on an upturned cask, and in the holders three candles guttered in the draft from the exit. Of the madwoman there was no sign!

Jane wriggled up into a sitting position and tested the strength of her bonds. They were quite strong, and it took her less than a moment to realise she stood little chance of wriggling out of them. But often in movies and books, the hero freed himself by holding his bound wrists in the candle flame — perhaps she could do so!

It took her several minutes to get to her feet and hop across the cellar. When she was near enough to the candles to push her tied wrists into the flames, she paused. It was bound to be painful — but not nearly as painful as what the old woman might do to her.

Clenching her teeth, Jane placed her bonds over the flame. Sharp, searing agony made her almost cry out. The flame licked round her hands, scorched her soft skin, and ran hungrily along her bare arms. With a sob she pulled away and tried the ropes again, but it was no use — they were as strong as ever, and she knew she could never stand the pain of the flames again. A hard sob escaped her and she slumped towards the floor.

Between two barrels facing her, a low wooden door which she had failed to notice previously suddenly opened. Through it came the madwoman — a truly shocking sight. The blood from her wounds had congealed on her grey wrinkled face; some of it had dripped onto her black dress and her hands. There was still that insane glare in her one good eye. Gazing at her terrible injuries, Jane found herself marvelling that the old woman had been able to stand up to all the punishment she'd had. Had she been sane, she could not have done so: but madness often brings with it a strange kind of strength — a strength of the mind over the body. In her claw-like hand she bore the cruel weapon with which she had already killed five — possibly six — people.

The woman seemed calmer now; her features were more composed as she laid the steel claw down beside the candles.

Jane tried to speak, and for a moment no sound came. Then she forced words from her dry throat: 'What — what have you done with — Bob?' she gasped.

The old woman glanced evilly across at her. 'The young man who was with you? He has gone! I saw him leave. I was in the library getting my little toy when he walked straight out. He will not help you.'

'Then you didn't kill him?' asked Jane in surprise.

'Kill him? No! Why should I? I have no quarrel with him. It is only my family I wish to kill!'

'Your … family? But — but you killed your husband — isn't that all the family you have?'

'Of course — you don't know, do you? Prepare yourself for a shock, woman! I am your Aunt Lucille Rivers — not Ashville's wife!'

Jane felt her head swimming wildly. 'My aunt's dead,' she stammered. 'You killed her — in the library … You're — you're mad.'

The old woman bared her teeth in a snarl. 'I *am* mad,' she grated. 'You and the rest of my fine family have made me so. You all conspired against me!'

'I don't understand,' Jane said faintly. 'Do you mean that you really are my Aunt Lucille?'

'Yes! The woman who was found in the library last week was Martha Ashville. But the fools thought it was I — as I meant them to think!' A cackle of hideous laughter burst from her blood-caked lips.

'But why, why?' demanded Jane, her curiosity subduing her terror.

'It's a long story, my dear Jane,' cackled Lucille Rivers mockingly. 'But since we have plenty of time, now that that interfering young man is not here, I will tell it to you. It may be that your late, lamented father — my brother — has not mentioned me much to you?'

'He — he didn't,' Jane said. 'That is — well — not much. He simply told us that you lived at Rivers End, but he never suggested going to see you or anything.'

'Why?' snapped the madwoman.

'He — he said you were . . . a little queer.'

Another peal of laughter rang through the cellar. 'He was right, my dear Jane. I was a little queer. Perhaps you think I still am, eh?'

Jane did not reply.

'Of course I am,' said the old woman. 'But I think that I am saner now than I have ever been since your grandmother — my mother — died. I don't suppose your father told you that, either, did he? He didn't tell you that shortly after your grandfather passed away, your grandmother had a paralytic stroke. She was confined to her bed eternally and had to be lifted, carried, nursed, fed, cared for. And he didn't tell you that out of all her children, I was the only one who stayed by her, looked after her, until the very end! All the others, your father included, left home and married; hardly bothered to even call and see their paralysed mother. But I stood my ground! For thirty weary years I cared for my mother, attending to her every want. I didn't mind, for I was young and strong in those days, and I loved her more than anything else.

'At last she passed on, and I was left alone. She had left me her entire fortune, and had entirely disinherited her other sons and daughters, which was no more than they deserved. But they were furious, both with her and with me. And when her death caused my reason to go for a short time, they had me put into an institution. Then they began to scheme to cheat me out of my inheritance. They got together and, while I was still ill, persuaded me to sign a paper nominating them as my trustees. I did so, and they drew out a will, depriving me of the right to leave my money to anyone I chose. The will stated that the money must pass to *their* issue, if I failed to have any children of my own. That was a remote possibility, for I was fifty-one when I left the institution.

'I was quite sane then, capable of judging things for myself, but I found that it was impossible to revoke the powers of trusteeship that I had given them by signing that form in the home. Twice I took the matter to court, but each time they produced a specialist who maintained that, while I was not a certifiable case, I was still mentally incapable of controlling my own affairs.

'My own brothers and sisters! Can you wonder that I was bitter? I had spent most of my life nursing my mother, losing my chances of marriage, and for what? They cut me off from my inheritance in every possible way. They allowed me practically nothing to live on. They set spies — Ashville and his wife — to watch me, to act as keepers, to see that I didn't try to marry. I might have married . . .' She broke off, a softer light in her eye. Then her voice hardened. 'But they contacted the man who had been good enough to ask for my hand and told him I was hopelessly insane! I never saw him again.

'A few months ago I knew I had not long to live. I could feel it. I hated Ashville and his wife; they were cruel to me — I think that living with them brought me to this state — and I was determined that if I were to die, they should; and also, that my remaining relatives and their children should not touch one penny of the money they had robbed me of!

'I spent weeks sharpening up five old knife blades and sewing them into a worn leather glove. Then one day I sent Ashville to town on some pretext. While he was gone, I took Martha by surprise and knocked her unconscious. Then I dressed her in my clothing, laid her in the library, and ripped her face until it was unrecognisable. She was about my height and build, and neither of us had any special distinguishing marks. I then took all the valuables I could find and hid them away, to make it seem as if Martha had murdered me and robbed the house. I had laid in a supply of food so that I could spend the time in the secret passages until the date of the will reading.

I knew that the will was to be read here — it has always been the custom in our family.

'The rest you know. I killed Mortimer first — I hated him more than any of the others. Then Esmeralda. Next Archie, and last … well, that will come shortly, Jane. Ashville I had meant to leave for last; but when he decided to go for the police, I had to make a quick end of him.

'You understand now, do you not, my dear Jane? You can see why you must die.'

'But I didn't have anything to do with cheating you,' said Jane desperately.

'Not directly. Neither did Archibald. Yet you would inherit my money through your parents' scheming, and I am determined that I will smash their plans at the last!'

'But, Aunt Lucille …' cried Jane.

'No use pleading. I must go through with it now. When you have been put to rest, I shall kill myself, and the Rivers fortune will go to the state, where it will be better used than if it fell into the family's hands.' She picked up the steel-tipped glove and slipped it onto her right hand.

'Not that — please,' sobbed Jane,

shrinking away.

'I shall not hurt you, Jane. I tried to kill Archibald as quickly as possible. Mortimer deserved to suffer — and so did Esmeralda——but my quarrel with you is indirect; therefore I shall make the end as quick as I can.' She started to advance towards the terrified woman, the gruesome glove held in readiness.

'Help — oh, Bob, help!' shrieked Jane.

'Don't be silly,' said Lucille Rivers. 'I have already told you the young man has left. Say your prayers, Jane.'

The knives came steadily nearer — nearer — poised above Jane's strained, ashen face. The hand that held them drew up for the stroke ...

10

The Night Is Ending

Bob blundered along the narrow passage; his torch, growing dim now, casting a feeble ray in front of him and marking his path. He was certain the cry he had heard came from Jane, and it was enough to warn him that she was in deadly peril.

At the bottom of the passage he could see a glimmer of light, seeming to come through a thin crack. Breathlessly he raced along to it, but going more quietly so as not to put the madwoman on her guard.

The light came from round the edge of a wooden door; and without hesitating, Bob pulled it open.

Lying on the floor, her pallid face illuminated by the light from three candles, was Jane. She was shrinking from the malevolent figure that stood above her like some monstrous bird of prey waiting for the final swoop. In the woman's hand was the ghastly instrument that had figured so largely in the night's events; and as Bob's eyes rested upon the scene, she was raising her hand to deliver the killing stroke!

Almost without thinking, Bob took aim and sent the heavy torch skimming through the air towards the old crone's head. It struck hard and square at the nape of her hunched neck, and with a startled screech she staggered sideways and collapsed onto the flagstones. But her shock was only momentary — for as Bob dashed towards Jane, the old woman had already started to scramble to her feet, the weapon still glistening in her hand. Her face was contorted with ungovernable fury, and unearthly snarls and whimpers tumbled through her yellow teeth.

Bob gave her one quick glance and knew that she would be on them before he had time to untie Jane. He knew also that unarmed as he was, he would suffer terrible disfigurement — possibly death — if he attempted to disarm the madwoman. Rapidly he picked Jane up as she was, turned, and ran for the cellar steps. As he passed the candles he knocked them to the floor with his elbow, plunging the cellar into darkness.

It was a weird sensation, staggering up those steps with a bound woman in pitch blackness, and with a madwoman gibbering and mouthing somewhere behind him. But finally he gained the door that led into the house proper, slid Jane to the floor, and turned and bolted the cellar door on the old woman. Then, and only then, did he pause to wipe the sticky perspiration from his aching brow.

He glanced down at Jane and found that the excitement and fear had been too much for her. She had fainted. He untied the rope that held her wrists and ankles and half carried, half dragged her towards the kitchen.

He was almost there when he realised that it would not take the madwoman long to make her way out of the cellar by the secret door. He therefore changed direction and, picking Jane up and holding her across one shoulder, made for the front door, flung it open, and ran out into the night.

The sudden impact of the drenching rain on her face made Jane regain her senses.

Bob set her down on a step and patted her check until she was fully aware once more.

'Bob! Thank heavens you came! She was going to kill me like she killed the others. And she isn't Ashville's wife at all — she's really my Aunt Lucille!'

'*Your Aunt?*' Bob was flabbergasted.

'Yes, Lucille Rivers. You see —'

'Tell me some other time,' Bon panted. 'We aren't out of the woods yet. The old devil will be after us shortly, I think, and on the whole the best plan would be to put as much distance as possible between ourselves and her!'

Jane nodded and gave a frightened glance at the front door, which Bob had slammed on the way out.

'Can you walk?' Bob asked.

She nodded.

'Good! Then have a shot at running!'

With his arm hooked under hers and helping her along, they began to run down the drive. They passed the library window, and by the aid of the almost continuous lightning, Bob had a momentary glimpse of the madwoman staring out at them, mouthing and screaming.

'Where can we go?' gasped Jane breathlessly, as they turned into the roadway. 'We — we can't possibly get to the village in all this!'

'No, we can't. I was thinking that if we could reach my car, we could spend the rest of the night in that. Your aunt may not venture out of the house. And if she does, I've got an extremely heavy jack-handle in the old Austin, so I'll be able to give her something to think about!'

They ran warily, and in silence, until they reached the Austin. Bob helped the exhausted woman into the rear seat and climbed in beside her.

'Oh, Bob,' Jane whispered. 'What would have happened to me without you?'

'It's not over yet,' replied Bob gloomily.

'Don't say that — please.'

'What a sucker I was,' Bob told her. 'I should have hared off when Ashville told me about the curse on strangers, if I'd had any sense at all.'

'It's a funny thing about that curse,' Jane said. 'Out of all the people in that house last night, you were the only one Aunt Lucille *didn't* want to kill.'

'If she didn't, she had a darned fine try,' countered Bob. 'The way she stroked my face with that claw of hers wasn't exactly affectionate.'

Bob had been fumbling under the rear seat and now he sat up again, clutching a heavy iron jack-handle. 'Now,' he said grimly, 'let her come down here, and I'll give her a right royal welcome, woman or not.'

He reached over and found the brandy, which he handed to Jane. She took it thankfully and drank some, then fell into a spasm of coughing and choking.

Meanwhile, Bob's eyes were fixed on the road ahead. Each time the forked lightning seared the dismal sky, he peered keenly up towards the old house. After about five minutes, he clutched Jane's arm tightly. 'Here she comes,' he murmured. 'Now hold tight, honey. Don't be scared — I'll be able to handle her all right this time!'

Thunder boomed overhead, and lightning flashed repeatedly, as Jane gazed in fascination up the road. Approaching at a shambling run, and still dressed only in her black gown, which now clung damply about her misshapen form, was her Aunt Lucille. On her right hand was the dreadful claw, and as she ran it was raised, waving towards the heavens. When she saw the car, she stopped and burst into a prolonged cackle of hideous laughter that was seized and swept away by the wind, lost in the tumultuous voice of the thunder.

Bob slid out of the car, gripping the jack-handle firmly, and stood in the road, ready to meet her.

As she saw this, the old woman began to creep towards the car, screaming and shouting horrible curses at the two of them. Step by step she advanced, until she was less than ten yards away. Then she stood upright, threw her face to the sky, and shrieked imprecations. Her steel-tipped hand waved furiously backwards and forwards. She gathered herself for a sudden run ... and then it happened!

A long, jagged fork of lightning streaked earthwards and struck the steel knives on the glove she wore. To Bob and Jane, it seemed to pour itself into her upraised arm. There was an immense flash of blue light and a blinding glare that caused them to shut their eyes tightly. Then it was over!

Lucille Rivers, charred and twisted beyond recognition, was sinking to the muddy ground . . . electrocuted.

* * *

A watery sun shone over the little village of Riverton. Here and there in the treetops an early bird or two tweeted, and the sound of boots began to make themselves heard along the cobbled streets. It had been a terrible storm, but it was over now, and Riverton was setting about the daily tasks.

The clip-clop of horses' hooves denoted the fact that the milkman was on his homeward way. And in the bar of the George and Dragon, Colonel Blumstead-Carrion (invariably an early riser) was just attacking his second plateful of ham and eggs and fried potatoes.

Through the rapidly drying puddles of rain, towards the only cab the village boasted, a small, insignificant little man wearing a black suit and tie, elastic-sided boots, and a pair of pince-nez, pushed his way. In addition to the above, he was also wearing a cheerful smile.

This was Mister Nathaniel Stimson, junior partner in the firm of Buddlewick, Buddlewick, Harringay and Stimson, solicitors and attorneys-at-law. Mr. Stimson was feeling pleased. He was making his way to Rivers End to read the will of the late Lucille Rivers to her family.

And the point was that this was the first time Nathaniel had been entrusted with a task of such magnitude. As a rule it fell to Buddlewick Senior, Buddlewick Junior, or Harringay. But happily Buddlewick Senior was confined to his home with a touch of lumbago, Buddlewick Junior was handling a more important matter, and Harringay was on his yearly holiday. So it had fallen to Mr. Stimson, whom they usually regarded as a sort of glorified office boy, to undertake the important task of reading the Rivers will.

He chirruped a cheery good morning to the ancient cabby, packed himself into the rear, and gave the address. The cabby started up, and with a grinding of gears got underway.

'Terrible night,' said Mr. Stimson brightly.

'Ay,' replied the cabby breezily.

'Must have been a lot of damage done,' observed the solicitor cheerily.

'Ay,' said the cabby vociferously.

'Caused me to miss an important appointment,' Mr. Stimson continued exuberantly. 'But fortunately it will do just as well this morning.'

'Ay,' drawled the cabby laconically.

'I expect they're all up there, waiting impatiently for me to arrive,' Mr. Stimson mused glowingly. He felt very important for the first time in his frustrated life.

'Ay,' said the cabby, who had never felt important, and was never likely to.

Finding that the man was not exactly the talkative kind, the solicitor allowed the conversation to lapse. Halfway up the hill they passed an Austin Seven, firmly embedded in a watery ditch.

'My word,' prattled Mr. Stimson, 'it looks as though there's been in accident.'

'Ay,' said the cabby stoically.

They turned into the drive of Rivers End, crawled past the library, and drew up outside the front door. Mr. Stimson alighted, and as he did so, the door opened and a young woman looked out.

'Miss Rivers,' the solicitor greeted her, beaming. 'How nice to see you again!'

'Hello, Mr. Stimson. Would you tell the cabby to wait a few minutes, please? I want him to drive Bob down into the village to get the police.'

'Bob? The — the police?' echoed Mr. Stimson.

He passed the instructions to the cabby.

'Ay,' said that worthy, unmoved.

Mr. Stimson clutched his briefcase and turned towards the house.

''Ere,' said the cabby, 'wot the 'ells the game? Six an' frippence yer owes me!'

'Tut, tut,' exclaimed the solicitor. 'I had quite forgotten the fare. Here's ten shillings, my man — you can keep the change.'

'Aye.'

'Sorry I was a little late,' said Stimson as he passed into the hall.

'You *were* a little late,' agreed Jane, 'but perhaps it's just as well for you that you were.'

'Eh?' said Stimson vaguely. He peered

round short-sightedly through his pince-nez. 'Might as well start at once, hey?' He chuckled. 'I suppose they're all eagerly waiting for me.'

'I wouldn't exactly say that,' Jane said with a wan smile.

'Where are the others? Miss Esmeralda, Master Archibald, and Sir Mortimer? I take it they are here, are they not?'

'Oh yes, they're here, Mr. Stimson. We put them in the library. You see —'

'Splendid, splendid. Where is the butler?'

'He's in the library, too. But you must *listen* to me —'

'Later, Miss Rivers, later. Mustn't keep my clients waiting, must I?'

'But you don't understand —'

'I will, I will,' said Stimson jocularly as he hurried towards the library.

'You certainly will,' breathed Jane, following him into the library, where the bodies of the dead had been laid out by Bob.

Bob, having finished his wash and brush-up in the bathroom, came skipping down the stairs, his face still bandaged. As he reached the last step from the direction of the library, he heard an audible thud. Jane hurried out, looking distressed.

'Now what?' demanded Bob wearily.

'Come in here, please. Hurry.'

'But I was just going for the limbs of the law. I saw the solicitor arrive in a cab — it was Stimson, wasn't it?'

'Yes,' Jane said. 'It was Stimson — but — he just *fainted*!'

Phantom Of Charnel House

1

The Charnel Estate

It was the middle of January, and the express train I was on was carrying me ever deeper into the heart of the English countryside. But not the English countryside we like to think of: green, rolling pastureland; winding silvery brooks; stately elms, oaks, beeches; the sunlight playing on whitewashed low-roofed farmhouses and buxom farmers' daughters; and herds of sheep, cows and horses grazing in sunny meadows adjacent to patches of sweet-smelling hay.

No.

This was the grim, fog-bound countryside of winter: the hard, dry earth; the gaunt, leafless trees; and the cottages huddled tightly together, as if seeking security from the iciness of the biting winds that whined and moaned across the moors.

For the last half hour of my journey, the train had been puffing asthmatically into a layer of mist that had gradually changed into a solid curtain of fog, concealing everything from view save the monotonous railings and embankments that tore past incessantly. The whirr and clatter of the locomotive sounded muffled and unreal; and the bitterness of the atmosphere penetrated into the first-class compartment I was in, making me shiver and turn up the collar of my coat.

There were no other passengers — the countryside draws few visitors in seasons like this — and I had the compartment to myself. My legs were stretched along the seat, a practice upon which the railway company would undoubtedly have frowned; and my head was crammed up against the window blind which I had drawn. Although the carriage was a nonsmoker, I had my old pipe in my mouth, and I was belching thick lungfuls of smoke into the chill air about me.

I had caught the train in a hurry, and had neglected to provide myself with any reading material. Accordingly I drew out, for the twentieth time, the letter that had brought me on this dismal winter journey.

It wasn't a long letter, and it was from a man I had been at Cambridge with, and who, until he had married recently, had been one of my closest friends. It simply said:

Dear Wenton,

How are you, old chap?

I'm afraid I've neglected to write you for some time, but really I've been so busy in my new business that I haven't had a chance. Besides, we both know ours isn't one of those friendships that have to rely on correspondence. I mean, no matter how long has passed without us seeing or hearing from each other, we can still pick up at the point where we left off, at any given moment.

So I'll be frank, perfectly frank, with you, Wenton. I'm writing now because I need your help! You know I invested all my capital in the Charnel Estate scheme. Well, unless something is done — unless you can help me — I'm ruined! You seem to have built up quite a reputation for yourself as a ghost hunter — I've read about you a great deal in the papers

— and if ever anyone needed a ghost hunter, Wenton, I'm the chap.

If you can't manage it, of course, it can't be helped. But I know that if you possibly can, you will, if only for the memory of our past association.

And if that doesn't move you, old chap, here's something to whet your appetite: this entire estate is haunted by a phantom!

Do try to get here as quickly as possible,

Always your old friend,

Walter Mason.

So that was it: he hadn't told me very much about his so-called phantom, but the little he had had whetted my curiosity all right!

Perhaps I should explain. About six years ago an old uncle of mine died, and I found myself heir to a considerable fortune, which made it no longer necessary to follow a career. I loafed about for a couple of years, but then I found time hanging very heavily on my hands, and I knew I should have to have some hobby.

I had always been interested in ghostly legends; so I inserted an advertisement in *The Times*, stating that a gentleman would be interested to hear of, and to investigate, any ghostly phenomenon, free of charge. The replies were amazing — apparently England was overrun with ghosts and would-be spirits.

I found the pastime fascinating, and went on investigating one case after another. In many I was able to 'lay' the ghost, and prove that the tappings, manifestations and hauntings were due to natural causes, or to unscrupulous persons with axes to grind. But once or twice I came up against cases that I was quite unable to solve: the vampire of Sutton, for instance, and the haunted castle of Vallepper in Austria. These I had reluctantly to acknowledge as genuine manifestations, although in my own mind I still retained doubts.

The result of all these pryings into the unknown was good copy for the papers; and they made full use of it, labelling me the Supernatural Detective, and even persuading me to pen a series of articles for them dealing with the occult.

I suppose it was one of these articles Walter Mason had seen, and in his troubles he had immediately decided to ask me down to try and lay his 'phantom'. So here I was, a few hours after receiving his letter, steaming down to the new Charnel Estate in bitterly cold weather. The fog, when the train finally decanted me at a small newly erected station, was almost intolerable. It lay thickly over the waiting room, and ethereal tentacles of the stuff wrapped themselves about my legs and drifted into my nostrils, bringing with them that damp, clammy stench of dead earth and wet grass, which caught at the back of my throat and made me cough harshly. So little could I see in front of me, that I almost fell down the flight of wooden steps from the platform to the main road.

I had wished to see a little of the Charnel Estate, but it was worse than useless in such a pea-souper. All I could make out were the flattish tops of small square houses, dimly visible through the greyness of the heavy fog.

I glanced about me for some conveyance, but found none. I grunted and began to walk along the street, hoping to come across some passer-by who would direct me to Walter's place, Charnel Lodge.

To my right, I could see blurs of light in the murkiness, and I made my way in that direction. There was a small public house with a swinging sign outside that read 'The Charnel Arms'.

I pushed open the brass-handled door and walked in. There were quite a number of men at the bar; and as I entered, they turned — almost fearfully, I thought — and stared at me as I crossed towards them.

'Good evening,' I said politely. It seemed to snap the tension that was gripping them, and one or two nodded to me. Then they resumed their drinks and their conversations in low tones.

I ordered a whisky and soda, and while I drank it thankfully, I listened to their talk. A few feet away from me was an old man who appeared to have a great deal to say. He was speaking in an ominous tone of voice and the others were listening, nodding every now and then.

'I'm tellin' ye,' said the old fellow, ''tis the real thing, so help us! What else could it be? Did not they come an' break down old Charnel House to make room for this estate? An' that bein' so, where would the phantom go? Nay, he's angry at bein' moved from where he's haunted all these many years, and he'll kill all who stay here! He'll not be content 'til the place is dead an' deserted, so he won't!' And the rest inclined their heads in gloomy agreement.

'Pardon me for intruding,' I said, causing them to spin in my direction, 'but did I hear you mention something about a — ghost?'

'That ye did, mister,' said the old fellow, nodding. 'The phantom of Charnel House!'

'But you don't really believe in such things? Not seriously!'

The old fellow went a little red, and I saw I had annoyed him. He said: ''Tis all right for you young fellows to be talkin' about not believing in such things. But me, I've lived here for nigh on fifty year, an even when we was kids we gave Charnel House a wide berth. It was haunted then, so help us, and now it's gone, the same phantom haunts this estate!'

'Oh come now.' I smiled. 'Possibly there may be a ghost as you say. But then again, isn't it possible that actually it's only some human agent trying to scare you all?'

There was a murmur of anger at this, and I regretted the rather blunt way I had put it.

'Human agent, is it, mister?' growled the manager from behind the bar. 'Well, maybe it is, and maybe it isn't. We don't scare easy round here, as you'd know if you wasn't a stranger. But this is too much for any man's nerves! Of an ordinary evening before this damned phantom scare got us, this bar would be crowded. Now look at it, and see if you think about two hundred men could be scared by any human agency, so much as to stop them having their nightly drink! These men here all live close to, otherwise they wouldn't have risked it — would you?'

Thus addressed, the company shook their heads vehemently.

'Perhaps, while you all join me in a drink, you'd like to tell me about it?' I suggested.

They looked at each other, then the manager nodded and said: 'If you're passing through here, I'll tell you for your own good! And when you've heard, you might have the sense to keep a sharp lookout in this place.'

The drinks were served up, and the manager began: 'You may know that this is all new property. There used to be nothing bar fields about here — except for old Charnel House. Charnel House — and it was a good name for it, too! It used to belong to a man called Roger Charnel, who built it back in the eighteenth century. Only, the things he did there were terrible. He used to run some sort of secret society, and he'd practise the black arts and make human sacrifices. Where he got his victims from, nobody rightly knew — but coaches that passed Charnel House would reach the next village empty, the passengers having mysteriously vanished on the way. The coachmen would go too; and the horses, from force of habit, would draw the empty coaches home, along the route they always travelled.

'People who got too near Charnel House at night often vanished, and others who didn't claimed they heard horrible shrieks coming from the cursed place. But any investigation always drew a blank, and Roger Charnel went about his hideous business until one night in December, 1765. Then, after the disappearance of some young maidens from the next village, the people there banded together and went to the home of Roger Charnel.

'It was such a night as has seldom been seen since history began: a howling blizzard was hurling icy snow down from a leaden sky, and the rough roads of that time were miniature quagmires. But the men pushed on, and came to Charnel House just as the shadows were falling. And they heard the screams!

'So they broke in. They were too late to save the women, for he had them hung against the wall of the cellar, and he had driven long steel harpoon-shaped weapons into their stomachs. Roger Charnel himself was covered by flowing black draperies, and his evil, contorted features were white and seemed to shimmer in the shadows of that damned cellar. He was a dwarf; and to make his appearance more nauseating, when they tore the cloak from him they also found his back frightfully hunched.

'They stripped him naked and carried him out into the blizzard. Then they built a pile of broken furniture from his mansion and laid him on the top and set fire to the pyre — there, in the middle of that wild December snowstorm.

'He cursed and shrieked, heaped maledictions on their heads and vowed to return, before the flames licked about his glimmering features. Then he was too busy shrieking with pain to curse his executioners further.

'After that there is only rumour to go on; but they say that all those men who had a hand in his death were found within the year, dying from wounds inflicted by a strange harpoon-like spear driven into their stomachs.

'Then nothing was heard; and for a long time, Charnel House was empty. But in 1860, a man and his niece went to live there. Two years later they found the niece murdered in the same way as Charnel had killed his victims. One of the harpoons, of which about twenty used to hang above the fireplace, was missing . . .

'The uncle was tried for the murder, and although he insisted the house was haunted and that the phantom of Roger Charnel had perpetrated the killing, he was not believed. The judge maintained that the legend must have preyed on his mind, eventually becoming an obsession, so that he had forgotten himself and killed his niece. On medical examination it was proved that he was insane: and he was committed to an institution for the remainder of his life. But there are those of us who believe that he was driven insane only through what he had seen and heard in Charnel House!'

'An intriguing story,' I said. 'But so far it hasn't been proved that there actually is any ghost! What happened to the place after that?'

'It was empty — nobody would buy or rent it,' said the manager. 'Not until about two years ago. Then a man called Mister Mason opened a factory hereabouts and purchased all of Charnel Estate to house his workers. He had Charnel House ripped down and modern houses put up on the site. His own home stands over what was originally Charnel House itself.

'Everything went smoothly for a time, although there were those who claimed he shouldn't have called the place Charnel Estate. But I suppose he let the original name remain because it was a sort of landmark that everyone knew. Just about six months ago the factory opened, and the workers poured into the five hundred houses Mason had built here. It was fine. There was a small cinema, a complete shopping district, and this pub. The whole place was self-contained, and Mason owned it all. It was shaping fair to make his fortune, until . . .

'Well, it really started three months ago with old Simon here seeing a figure late one night — a figure that lurked in the shadows, and which snarled at him as he drew near. It was dressed in floating black draperies, and its fingers were long and claw-like. Its face was horrible, he said, shimmering white and screwed up into a mask of hate. In its hand was a weapon shaped like a harpoon.' He turned to the old man I had been speaking to previously and said: ‘Tell him what you did, Simon!’

‘I ran like ’ell,’ said Simon frankly. ‘When I seen it stood there, all white an’ evil-lookin’, I says: ’Oo the ’ell are you?’ Then it took a step towards me, an’ I could see it was a dwarf and its back hunched up — an’ like a shot I knew it was the phantom of Charnel House, what had been thrown out of its home, as it were, and was now wandering the entire estate! It came for me with that weapon in its hand, an’ I picked up my feet and ran — I’d been a ruddy fool if I ’adn’t!’

‘Then other people saw it,’ went on the manager. ‘Lots of them. It got so’s the women folk wouldn’t even open the door after dark! I saw it, and Jake here saw it. Harry Richards and Mr. Mason himself! Some of the folks here packed up and left, but most of us decided to stay on because it was comfortable here, and we had good jobs, and Mason’s a regular fine fellow to work for. And it hadn’t touched anybody … not so far …’

I ordered another whisky, thoughtfully, and sipped it. The conversation seemed to have died away; and when the landlord looked like reopening it, old Simon growled: 'Shut up, Bob, you give me the willies!'

'By the way,' I told them, 'I myself am going to Mr. Mason's home; he expects me. Could anyone direct me?'

'None of us'll go with you, I don't think,' said the manager, 'and it'll be hard to find in this fog. But if you keep right on along this road and turn first right, you can't miss it. It's a big house — three times as big as any other here.'

'Thanks,' I said. 'And thanks for the story — it's been very interesting.'

And then, as they all nodded good-night, the scream came!

It came from somewhere outside, throbbing and shrilling through the grey murkiness of the fog; muffled, but vibrating with horror and pain! Like petrified men, we stood there, unable to move or stir for the moment. Then it came again, louder, clearer; and with the landlord on my heels and two others behind him, we made a dash for the door.

We were out — out in that thick, impenetrable fog — and the screams, quieter now, seemed to come from immediately opposite us.

I led the way across that gloomy road, and was the first to see the black shadow against the greyness — first to see the grinning, contorted, maniacal features glimmering with a ghostly white glow. The head was yellow, bare and bald, and that also was limned in a strange incandescence. The crooked fingers were stretched out in the fog, seeming to beckon. A ghastly cackling laugh issued from the spectre's mutilated lips, revealing a row of rotting teeth. Its eyes burned into mine with fierce intensity.

I glanced behind to see if the others were with me. They weren't! One look at that diabolic gloating face had been enough for them. I could dimly hear their footfalls as they ran back to the public house.

When I turned, the phantom was dimming, vanishing into the fog. His features had become blurred and indistinct and his mocking laugh was fainter. I clenched my teeth and threw myself forward — my flying feet stumbled over something soft, unseen in the fog — and then I was sprawling on hands and knees, and any chance of catching the phantom was gone . . . if it were possible to catch him at all!

I regained my feet, and my startled eyes fell on the thing I had tripped over. It was the body of a young man, and as he writhed in agony I could see the handle of a strange weapon protruding from the blood and gore that soaked his shirt just above his stomach!

Even as I bent towards him, his moaning and writhing ceased, and the death rattle rasped from his tortured throat.

2

Again, the Phantom!

It was almost two hours before I managed to get along to Walter's place. They were spent in assisting the men from the Charnel Arms to carry the body into the public house; in accompanying the landlord while he went for the police; in going down to the small police station and being interrogated by a red-faced sergeant, who was evidently as fearful of the phantom as the people he was supposed to guard; and finally, in renewing old acquaintanceship with Walter Mason himself, whom the sergeant had sent for.

He looked much the same as when I had last seen him, except for a trace of iron grey in his hair, which he assured me he had not had two months previously. His features were still handsome, though more lined than I recalled; and his welcome, if subdued because of the circumstances, was no less hearty. He identified the dead man as one of the night watchmen at his factory, and assumed that he had been on his way to take over his shift at the time of his unfortunate meeting with the phantom.

The sergeant telephoned Scotland Yard, and the Yard promised to send along a man first thing in the morning. And then we were free to go, and in Walter's car we drove the half mile or so to his home.

It was a modern — what I term geometric — house, full of unexpected curves and hard angles. Lights were blazing into the fog from the downstairs windows, and as soon as Walter had garaged the car we entered the house.

I was quickly introduced and made at home. There was only Walter himself, his wife — whom I knew slightly — and his wife's sister, Angela, a charming woman of about twenty-two. I must confess that from my sight of Angela Brent, I was more than interested! She was the possessor of beautiful features, and her glossy black hair framed her small oval face, contrasting pleasantly with the full redness of her lips. Her figure was perfect; and the tight-fitting yet simple dress she wore enhanced it. Her slim legs were clad in sheer silk stockings.

She greeted me with a grave smile and the remark: 'At last I meet the great Wenton Morland!'

'Not *really* great.' I smiled.

'Perhaps not that — but certainly resourceful, if we are to believe what we read about you, Mr. Morland,' she rejoined.

We went in to a cold supper which Annabelle, Walter's wife, had laid for us, since the two servants were already in bed.

'You see, Wenton,' explained Walter frankly over the table, 'I sank all my money into the factory and this estate for the workers' homes. And now that this damned phantom's started up business here, the workers are leaving me — leaving the factory and their homes, in fear of what might happen to them! Nor can I replace them; the public have got wind of the haunting and no one cares to come here now. Unless you can stop this spectre — or whatever it is — I'm absolutely ruined!'

'I can see that, Walter,' I said sympathetically. 'Well, suppose we go about this thing in a logical way, and instead of assuming that all that's been going on here is supernatural, let's just work on the grounds that there *is* a reason for it. The harpoon, for a start: where did it come from?'

'I feel sure it's one of the twenty or so that hung in Charnel House before we pulled the place down.'

'Good! Then taking that as a matter of fact, let's try and get to the bottom of this thing by working out who could have got hold of those harpoons.'

'I don't know that; I wasn't here when the workmen took the place down. But Weyland will know.'

'Who's Weyland?' I asked.

'He's my fiancé,' put in Angela, and I felt a sudden pang of annoyance. Why, I could not exactly say; only that I had been taking it for granted that she was unattached and that we would have several pleasant evenings together.

'And he's my surveyor,' went on Walter. 'A fine young chap, one of the best. Angela couldn't do better than marry him. He attended to all the laying out and planning of this estate for me, and at present he's working on improvements to the factory.'

'And he was in charge when the old house came down?'

'He was.'

'Hmm. Can we get in touch with him, do you think?'

'Naturally. He happens to be staying with us — where is he, Angela?'

'He went to the cinema, Walter. I wouldn't go because of the weather.'

'Then he should be back any moment. I expect he'll have heard what's happened to poor Robbins.'

We talked on, shelving the matter of the harpoons for a time.

'Is there anyone hereabouts who — I know it sounds rather fantastic — but who might be nursing a ... well, a grievance against you, Walter?' I asked.

I knew by his eyes, immediately, that there was. He hesitated to reply for a moment; then he smiled and said: 'Well, yes, in a way. But I hardly imagine he'd go to that extent. He's a funny sort of fellow, and he imagines I once did him dirt in a business deal. I needn't tell you I didn't, Wenton, but it's become a fixation with him. Whenever we meet, he invariably ignores me, and I believe he's tried to poison the minds of some of my men against me.'

'That seems a bit thick. Why don't you turf him out if the estate belongs to you?'

'I can't, and I'm not sure I would if I could. He doesn't live in one of the houses I built — he has a small mansion on the outskirts of the town, and it's his own property.'

We were interrupted by the slamming of a door, and a cheerful voice called: 'Hello! Where is everybody?'

'In here, Bob,' shouted Angela, and the door opened to admit a clean-limbed, fresh-faced young man of twenty-five or -six. He came in breezily and hurled himself — no other expression really describes the action — into an easy chair. Then he saw me, and made a movement to rise again.

'This is Mr. Morland,' said Walter. 'Wenton, this is Bob Weyland.'

We shook hands cordially, and Weyland smiled and said: '*The* Wenton Morland?'

'Really,' I pleaded, 'I'm beginning to feel quite notorious tonight. Everyone appears to have heard of me!'

'I should say we have,' said Weyland with a grin. 'Why, we've heard nothing else from Walter ever since this blessed phantom began to strut his stuff. Glad to see you down here, Morland.'

'You heard about Robbins?' questioned Walter.

'Robbins! What about Robbins?'

'Then you don't know Robbins was killed tonight?'

'Killed? Good God, no! I told you it was dangerous to leave that lower staircase at the factory open! I told the men to steer clear of it, until a door could be fixed —'

'It wasn't that, Bob,' said Walter wearily. 'Robbins was murdered; it wasn't any accident! He was killed by — the phantom!'

'You're joking, Walter.'

'No, I'm not joking. Wenton here found him, near the Charnel Arms. He had had one of those infernal harpoons driven into his stomach.'

Bob Weyland's hands clenched, but he said nothing.

I said: 'That's what we were talking about when you arrived. We wish to ask you if you can remember a thing or two that might help.'

'Ask on, by all means. If I can help in any way, I certainly will.'

'Thank you. I understand you were present when the old house was destroyed?'

'The Charnel House? Yes.'

'Perhaps you could recall what happened to the harpoons that were hanging above the fireplace?'

He knitted his brows and bit his lower lip. 'Let's see ... All the stuff was brought out into the grounds to be picked up by the auctioneers for delivery to their London rooms ... There were quite a lot of workmen about. Do you think someone stole them?'

I shook my head. 'We were hoping you might have noticed someone hanging about.'

'No, no one in particular. Actually, there were easily twenty men who might have pilfered them, I suppose. Oh, yes, I did notice one stranger — at least, he was to me at the time. Alec Gregory from the Elms.'

'Gregory?' echoed Walter. 'Why, that's the man I was telling you about, Wenton! The fellow who nurses an imagined grievance!'

'That's interesting,' I said.

'If I thought for a minute ...' began Walter, but I shook my head at him and smiled.

'Let's not jump to conclusions, my friend,' I said. 'Did you see anyone else, Weyland?'

'Only old Simon from the village — oh yes, and Leslie Stomberoff.'

'He's by way of being the village idiot,' explained Walter. 'No harm in him. He used to be quite a big name in the theatre, until a piece of heavy scenery fell one night and struck him on the head. He, like Gregory, owns his own property, and he's quite a character about these parts. He's continually putting on an act!'

We argued this way and that for almost an hour. Then I knocked my pipe out, and Walter suggested bed. I was shown to a small but scrupulously neat room. After I had said my good-nights, I swung the window open, being more or less a fresh-air fiend. The damp, smelly, clammy fog oozed in, and I swung it closed again, preferring to be suffocated in my sleep rather than face that.

My room was on the ground floor; and as I stood at my window I could see the trim, well-tended garden, just discernible through the murk. I lit a final pipe, smoked it out, disrobed, and climbed under the sheets.

I don't know what woke me; it was pitch dark, and clearly I had been asleep for some time. I strained my eyes to become used to the gloom, and peered questingly about my bedchamber.

Then I saw it: white, glimmering, malignant, not six feet from my bed! As before, its face was halfway between a grin and snarl; and from its throat issued that gloating cackle. In its yellowed hands was clutched a — harpoon!

Like lightning I had made up my mind: if this were some supernatural visitation I would find out for certain, or die in the effort. And with that thought I acted, hurling myself from the bed and shouting aloud for help at the same time.

The ghostly visitant seemed to float backwards; his face contorted into a leer as I came at him. Then somehow he was through the door, and it had closed behind him. My head smashed against the woodwork with paralysing force, and I flopped, only half conscious, to the floor.

I was still dazed when the lights were switched on, and I became aware of Walter, Annabelle and Angela standing over me in attitudes of consternation.

'Good heavens!' cried Annabelle. 'What happened, Wenton?'

I told them as briefly as I could, and as I finished we were joined by Weyland.

'You're absolutely certain you weren't dreaming?' asked Walter.

I might have taken offence at this, but I shook my head.

'But all the doors and windows are locked! I attend to them personally!'

'Nevertheless, I wasn't dreaming,' I insisted.

'That's right, he wasn't,' agreed Bob, and I shot him a grateful look. 'I heard him yell, slipped on my dressing gown, and came hurrying out. I spotted a black shadow in the passage and followed it along towards the rear of the house.'

'You did?' Walter said. 'Then there *was* a door unlocked?'

'There was no door unlocked — laugh if you wish! The phantom vanished through the solid wall!'

3

The Great Stomberoff

Miraculously, the fog had cleared away by the following morning. There was even a little sunshine in evidence, and early in the day I took a solitary stroll through the new estate. There was little of interest; the houses were arranged in orderly rows, and were in three distinct sizes: one size for single men, one for couples, and a larger size again for those with families. Beyond the neat little avenues, as a sort of background — not only to the estate, but also to the entire lives of the tenants — rose the sheet-glassed front of Walter Mason's modern factory.

The people living and working here owed much to their employer. Mason's factory was the most modern, up-to-date affair in England; and the working conditions, I understand, were second to none. Each employee held a certain number of bonus shares, and when much work was turned out, they received a handsome dividend on their holdings. And this was the estate, the factory, and the man who would be ruined by this accursed phantom, unless …

I was standing idly by the Charnel Arms, watching the stream of workers go past, when I felt a light tap on my shoulder; and, turning to see whom it might be, I was aware of the smiling, fresh face of Bob Weyland. He carried a sheaf of papers under his arm, and was undoubtedly on his way to the factory.

'Hello, Wenton,' he said amiably. 'Weighing things up?'

'As a matter of fact, I was. It all seems very far away from the happenings of last night, doesn't it?'

'It does,' he agreed, frowning. 'But just study the faces of these people going down to the works!'

I did so, and I immediately saw what he was driving at. There was no good-natured early-morning banter between them as there always is between factory workers. They hurried silently past, eyes staring in front of them, some gazing fearfully at the dark stain on the pavement where Robbins had ended his life the previous night. Little knots of men walked by, talking in low undertones; and in all faces one thing was apparent: foreboding!

These people were afraid! They wanted to know who would be next — if there *was* a next.

'It's hit them damned hard,' continued Bob Weyland. 'The foreman tells me that sixteen came round to his place early this morning and told him they were leaving at once! And they have. In a way, you can't blame people if they lack the guts to stick and see a thing through.'

I could only nod silently. Without any doubt, the panic was on. I could visualise it continuing until there were no workers left, and Walter was compelled to close down his great factory.

I was suddenly aware of a tall, thin, elongated figure coming in our direction. I stared in surprise, for it was really a most unusual spectacle. He was an old gentleman of perhaps sixty, dressed in shabby top hat, cloth coat with moth-eaten fur collar, tight stove-pipe trousers, and elastic-sided boots! An ebony stick tapped the ground smartly as he came, two piercing grey eyes peered out from a weather-lined face, and his white locks floated in wisps from beneath his hat brim. His gloves were now dirty, but had once been mustard yellow.

'So!' he boomed in a deep fruity voice, coming to a standstill beside us. 'So it is you, my young friend, Weyland? Prithee, what is't this bright and sunny morn that makes yonder peasants slink like wounded jackals into those mighty portals yonder?' And he indicated, with a dramatic finger, the factory gates.

Bob Weyland grinned, and turning to me, winked. He said: 'Mr. Morland, I would like you to meet that fine actor, Leslie Stomberoff!'

'The Great Stomberoff!' boomed our companion. 'Idol of the masses — now restin', Mr. Morland. Tell me, sir, could you be an agent, come to offer me a part fitted to my great talents?'

'I'm sorry, Mr. Stomberoff,' I said apologetically, 'I'm afraid not.'

'Forsooth!' thundered he. 'Why do they

all forsake me? Once I was the hero of the music hall, the star of every production! Now, alas, they spurn me, cast me aside, like an old glove!'

Bob Weyland winked at me again and said: 'Well, I'll push along, Wenton. Cheerio!' He moved towards the gates, leaving Stomberoff and me together outside the Charnel Arms.

'Gad!' ruminated Stomberoff. ''Tis a sorry thing that they do not open the doors of yonder edifice before eleven-thirty of the clock!'

'It is, indeed.' I smiled. 'I myself could do with a snifter.'

'A snifter, sir? Pray, what is that? Ah, I see. I see it all! You crave a drink?'

'That's certainly one way of putting it,' I agreed.

He sucked the handle of his stick pensively. 'They tell me murder was done here yester e'en. Is it so?'

'I'm afraid it is,' I said, nodding.

'Hmm! Would that I could meet this phantom, this foul wraith, this fiend in human guise! I would smite him hip and thigh with my good cane!'

‘You believe, then, that that would have any effect?’

‘Effect? Dam’ me, sir, of course it would! This phantom is a thing of flesh and blood, if ever there was one! I know, sir!’

‘And how do you know that, Mr. Stomberoff?’

‘It was the night I saw him … He was in front of me and ’twas mightily dark. He heard me not at first, and all that I could fain see was the back of his unlovely cloak. I heard him barge into a small tree, of which several line these roads, and he said: ‘Damn and blast these confounded trees!’ Was that the remark of a phantom, noble sir?’

‘It certainly wasn’t,’ I told him. ‘What happened then?’

‘I thought,’ said Stomberoff moodily, ‘that he was an agent, come to offer me a part in some gigantic production. I hailed him; and when he turned, I confess I was, for the nonce, stunned by the malign appearance of his physiognomy. When I had regained my wits, sir, he had fled. Aye! Fled, like some foul fiend of the night; fled from my presence, in such manner that I even thought he had vanished into air. But on closer and more profound observation, I was able to discern that he had merely fled down a side street.'

'You are sure all this is correct?' I asked him.

He stared at me haughtily and boomed: 'Do you dare to doubt my veracity, sir?'

'No, no, of course not. I merely wished to ascertain —'

He waved his stick imperiously, placed his free hand across that region of his waistcoat which presumably concealed his heart, and said: 'You have my word, good sir! The word of a Stomberoff!' Then he dropped his pose, glanced all round, leaned nearer to me, and whispered: 'They all think I am mad here. They are wrong! I am not mad! You can see that, can you not, sir?' And without waiting for any reply, he went on: 'Shall I tell you the truth? I, Stomberoff, am sane! But everybody else here is mad — raving mad!'

He suddenly whipped off his hat and made a swipe at nothing. 'Butterflies,' he said childishly. 'In winter! Most unusual, to say the least! I must secure one! Good day, sir,' he said courteously, and progressed down the street, making futile swipes at the empty air. As he went, there drifted back to me the strain of 'To be — or not to be? That is the question! Whether 'tis nobler in the mind to endure ...' His ponderous voice died away as he turned the corner and vanished from my sight.

I wandered idly back towards Walter's home and partook of a late breakfast. Annabelle was still in bed, having been terribly upset by the death of Robbins, whose widow she knew well; and now that the excitement was past, the strain had told on her fragility. Walter had gone down to the factory to see the foreman about the men who had left so rapidly, and I breakfasted with Angela.

It was extremely cosy, just the two of us alone there. Angela, who didn't seem to be a woman who was particularly worried about the proprieties of anything, was attired simply and sweetly in a diaphanous negligee with a sheer silk nightdress beneath.

'Aren't you rather afraid to trust yourself alone with such a man as I, in an outfit like that?' I chaffed her.

Her deep, liquid eyes censured me over the rim of her coffee cup. She said: 'Mr. Morland, you have a nice fatherly face. I would trust you anywhere!'

'A remark like that is what I asked for,' I said somewhat ruefully. 'Tell me, do I really look so — fatherly?'

She laughed — a tiny, tinkling laugh. 'No, of course you don't, Wenton! You don't mind me using your first name?'

'Not as long as you permit me the liberty of using your first name also, Angela.'

'I'd love you to. No reason why we shouldn't be good friends. I think it's so silly for people to call each other by formal names … kind of mid-Victorian rather, isn't it?'

'I hadn't really thought of it — but yes, I dare say it is.'

'You know, when Walter said he was sending for you, I visualised you as a middle-aged stuffed shirt. I did really!'

'And you weren't disappointed?'

'On the contrary, I *was* disappointed! I would rather you had been an old stuffed shirt, Wenton. You see, I must admit that what I have read about you makes me feel a queer sort of fascination. On top of that, you're young, handsome — oh, please don't blush! — and awfully good company. In other words, Wenton, you're a disturbing influence — and disturbing influences always upset me.'

'Exactly the same applies in my case,' I said. 'Imagine my surprise when I had expected only to see Walter and his wife, and you popped up! I was quite excited about it all until I heard you were engaged.'

'That's nice of you, Wenton. I'm not really engaged, of course. You will probably have noticed I am wearing no ring. But it's a generally accepted fact that I will marry Bob.'

'Generally accepted?'

'Exactly. Generally accepted by Walter and Annabelle — and Bob himself! In fact, the only one who hasn't entirely resigned herself to the idea is me!'

'You mean you aren't keen on it?'

'I didn't say that, Wenton, but I suppose that's what it boils down to. I haven't really met many other men besides Bob. Until now, Bob was the only man I'd met who had appealed to me in any way at all.'

'Until now?'

'That's quite correct, Wenton.'

'And what am I to assume from that, Angela?'

She looked me directly in the eyes, a mysterious half-smile on her lips, which were slightly parted. She said slowly: 'Assume whatever you wish.'

'I can only assume one thing,' I told her, 'and that is that you're a good flirt, and are having a little fun at the expense of a poor old ghost-breaker!'

She was about to reply, when the maid tapped on the door and said: 'Detective-Inspector Bristol to see Mr. Morland!'

4

Exit Alec Gregory

Detective-Inspector Bristol was a huge, bulky, ungainly man with a selection of double chins. He moved ponderously into the room; and as Angela rose to go, his eyes took in her flimsy attire. They remained phlegmatic, however; no flicker of interest stirred on his pasty white features. Angela blushed a little and rose to leave, but Bristol waved her back to her seat and said in a rich, throaty tone: 'Don't bother to go, miss. I won't detain Mr. Morland a minute.'

'Sit down, Detective-Inspector.' I smiled, giving him his full title, but he shook his ponderous head again.

'I merely want the details of what occurred, Mr. Morland. I understand you found the body . . .?'

I nodded, and briefly explained exactly what had happened to date, including my late-night visitor; my suspicions regarding Walter's old enemy, Gregory; and the opportunity Stomberoff would have had to secure the harpoons. 'We've looked up the auctioneer's inventory of the stuff they took from Charnel House,' I finished, 'and we found that there is no record of them having taken the harpoons. That means they were stolen prior to the van's arrival. And Weyland vouches for it that besides the workmen, there was no one about except Gregory and Stomberoff.'

'I think you're jumping to unwarranted conclusions,' said Bristol shortly. 'I've heard of you, Mr. Morland, and I've also heard of your peculiar talents. But I'm convinced they won't be needed on this case. I'll eat my police badge if this phantom isn't a thing of solid flesh and blood.'

'If I can assist you in any way, Inspector ...?'

'You can,' he said in a surly tone, 'by staying out of harm's way! I detest you amateurs messing about with jobs that would be better left to the official force!'

I retired, crushed. 'Very well, Inspector. Nice of you to put it so tactfully!'

He grunted, swung on his heel, and retreated to the doorway. As the door shut behind him, he said: 'Good day.'

For some seconds after he had gone I was motionless and speechless, gazing at the closed door. Angela broke into my thoughts by saying: 'What an awful man! I had no idea detective-inspectors were picked for their rudeness and uncouthness!'

'Neither had I,' I told her, 'until now! He seems to be the worst I've ever met so far. Most of the Yard men are only too glad to have a hand on a strange case like this! Ah, well, I won't let it bother me.'

'Or stop your own investigations?'

'Certainly it won't do that. Anybody has a right to solve crimes — that's something the police can't stop! And they can go to hell if they imagine I'll stand down simply because a fat, overbearing windbag orders me to!'

I must confess I was rather nettled by the attitude the plump official had taken. I felt it had made me look foolish in front of Angela, and that was the last thing I wished to happen.

The rest of the day passed pleasantly;

and shortly after we had dined at seven, I picked up my hat and coat and went out into the clear moonlit night. It was a vastly different night to the foggy one in which I had arrived; and Charnel Estate, despite its unhealthy name, looked calm and peaceful under the rays of the wintry moon.

I lingered about for a time, and soon afterwards Angela, well wrapped up against the cold, joined me. She said: 'Now what, Mr. Morland?'

'First of all,' I told her, 'let's get one thing straight! I thought we agreed to call each other by our first names? I mean when you call me Mr. Morland, it strikes me that I've slipped back in your estimation.'

'I forgot.' She smiled. 'All right —Wenton, then! You were very mysterious when you asked me to join you out here. Any reason?'

'Only that I felt Bob might get jealous.'

She laughed a little. 'Don't be absurd! Bob hasn't a jealous bone in his body! And besides, I do as I please and not as he pleases!'

'That's nice to know. I wonder if you'd be pleased to do something for me?'

'That depends,' she replied teasingly.

'Oh, it's only a matter of taking a walk with me. I'd like you to show me to Alec Gregory's place, if you will; I wish to have a word or two with him. I suppose you know him well enough to introduce me?'

'Why, of course. I thought it was something more personal you wanted ...'

'It may be — later on.' I grinned. 'Shall we start?'

It was an enjoyable walk to Gregory's mansion on the outskirts of the estate. We did it slowly, Angela's arm tucked through mine; and as we walked we talked of our interests, and were pleased to find we had much in common.

Neither of us referred to the flirtatious passage of the morning, and I began to think that possibly Angela *had* only been flirting after all; and that her interest in me was no deeper than the interest of any woman her age in a man who had built a reputation for himself as a ghost hunter.

Gregory's mansion was accessible only by a long tree-girt driveway, darkened by the shadows of massive, ancient elms, and I understood now why his place was so called. A house that was set literally in the middle of such a forest of trees could hardly be named anything other than The Elms.

We reached a gloomy, imposing façade, trod up a short flight of steps, and rang the bell by means of the worn bell rope. For some time there was no reply, and Angela informed me that Gregory lived alone and might possibly be in the back of the house. Finally, after repeated peals of the bell, the door was unchained and opened slightly; and the face of an aged, wizened man peered out at us.

'Ah,' he said, without much cordiality. 'Miss Brent.'

'Good evening, Mr. Gregory.'

'I fail to see what can bring you to my humble home. If it's anything connected with that damned brother-in-law of yours, you can go back to him and tell him I said he can go to hell! I happen to know he's been talking of prosecuting me for slander, and it doesn't interest me! All I say about him is true, and if he wishes he can take me to court and I'll stand up and say it there!'

'It's nothing to do with Walter, Mr. Gregory. This gentleman here would like to ask you a few questions — concerning the phantom!'

I watched him closely as she spoke, but his face betrayed little of his feelings. He opened the door wider and said with a surly grunt: 'All right. Come in!'

He led us into a small sitting-room on the right, poked at a dying fire, and said: 'I suppose you're from the police?'

I saw no reason to disillusion him. I nodded and said: 'That's correct, sir. Inspector Baker of the Yard.'

'What did you wish to ask me? I have quite a lot of work to do, you know, and I'd like you to make this interview as brief as possible.'

'It concerns the harpoons that used to hang in the old Charnel House. I understand you were on the spot when the place was pulled down; and I wondered if you had noticed those harpoons, and if so whether you could tell me anything about them.'

His eyes shifted from my face to Angela's, but again I was compelled to admit to myself that there was nothing guilty in his look. 'So that's the angle you're working on, is it? Yes, I did see the harpoons lying in a bunch, but I'm afraid I couldn't tell you who took them.'

'You are sure of that?'

'Certain.'

I saw no reason for prolonging the visit. My object in going at all had only been to see the man, and I had no real hopes that I should learn anything new. I rose to my feet and he to his.

'How are you getting on?' he asked as he escorted us to the door.

'Nicely, thank you! We expect to effect an arrest within twenty-four hours!'

Again his face told me nothing. He sniggered and said: 'That's what you policemen always say when you haven't the remotest idea of who committed the crime! Besides, I myself am certain that the phantom is supernatural — and it would be funny, I think, to see a ghost in the dock! Couldn't very well hang him, could you?'

'I am equally certain that the phantom is no ghost,' I said. 'However, we shall see.

Thanks for answering my questions.'

'One moment,' he said. 'Before you go, I shouldn't like to let you think you had made a fool of me! I happen to know you aren't any policeman, young fellow! I've seen your picture in the papers. You're that ghost hunter fellow, Morland. That's why I let you in in the first place, for I thought it would be rather interesting to hear what you had to say. It hasn't been. I wish I could have helped you further, but if I could I'm not sure that I would have done so! You see, I know this phantom is ruining Walter Mason. And I'm glad — glad, do you hear? I hope the phantom carries on with his work until Mason is broken and finished. You can tell him that from me!' Then the door slammed behind us.

I looked at Angela ruefully.

'He *is* a crusty old stick.' She smiled. 'But anyway, you've seen him now. What do you think?'

'I don't really know. He seems extremely cunning, and he certainly has it in for your brother-in-law.'

We commenced to tramp down the drive under the shadow of the elms. Suddenly

Angela's grip tightened on my arm, and she pointed to the side of the path and said: 'Did you see that? Amongst the trees!'

I looked but saw nothing. I shook my head.

'It was a — a sort of black shadow, moving towards the mansion! Do — do you think . . .?'

'I don't know — but we'll find out quickly enough!'

We retraced our steps cautiously towards the mansion, but we had hardly covered half the distance when screams — similar to those I had heard the previous night — began to issue from the darkness ahead. Running blindly, I tore along the drive, Angela a few feet in the rear. As I went I took the precaution of wrenching from my pocket the revolver I had placed there in readiness.

The front door was locked as we had left it, and for a moment I stood nonplussed. Then I turned and raced stumblingly round the side of the building.

Then I saw it again!

The phantom!

It was standing, leering, outside a small

porch that rose over the back entrance. As I rounded the corner, it began to glide rapidly away into the shadows. Once in those trees I would never find it; so, tensing my nerves, I raised my gun and took careful aim . . . The gun spat flame; and the bullets — three of them, one after another — sped straight towards their target.

It was as if they had missed entirely!

The figure wavered for a moment. Then it was gliding on; and from the shadows under the trees floated back that insane cackling laughter!

I stood petrified as Angela came round the house and joined me. 'Wenton . . . are you all right? The shots I heard . . .'

Even at that moment I was pleased to note that her face was strained and anxious, and her voice trembled. Clearly she was worried for my safety. I said jerkily: 'They were shots from my gun. I fired at the phantom.'

'Did — did you — hit him?'

'I *must* have done! But I can't understand — he just glided on into the trees, and I'm afraid I've lost him again. How could anything normal carry on with three bullets inside it?'

'Look,' said Angela. 'The door!'

I looked, and saw that the back door was staring wide open. From the interior of the house came a low blubbering sound. Fishing my torch from my pocket, I moved quickly inside. A long passage ran straight to the front door, and the moans came from the room we had so recently left. I pushed open the door and went in.

Alec Gregory was lying in a pool of his own blood on the floor. His eyeballs were protruding from his head, and his stomach was in a ghastly mess. The harpoon had been plunged home and savagely wrenched out again, and his intestines were showing, torn and mutilated.

I crossed over and knelt down by his side. His lips opened to frame a remark. He mumbled: 'I did see — someone — who was very interested in — those — harpoons. I — wasn't going to say — anything, for I — thought that I would get my revenge on — Mason by holding my — silence. But he must have known I saw him — and — he must have ...'

His head fell lack limply, and I stood up.

'Is he — dead?' asked Angela shudderingly, averting her eyes from the horror.

'Not quite dead yet — but I'm afraid he will be before we can get him to hospital. I don't think he'll regain his senses, either. A pity — there's something he could have told us.'

5

Exit Stomberoff!

'Very funny, it all is,' rumbled Detective-Inspector Bristol, chewing a matchstick and eyeing me as if I would have a lot of explaining to do. 'Very funny, altogether! How is it, Mr. Morland, that you have a rare penchant for being on the scene of the crime each time it happens?'

'Perhaps it's because I'm not quite as *thick* as the police, and can manage to see a bit further than the end of my nose,' I snapped back, remembering how rude he had been that morning.

He sniffed a little and threw the matchstick away. 'Really, Mr. Morland? That doesn't alter the fact that there are two dead men on this estate, and that you found them both! Isn't that rather strange?'

'Not as I see it,' I retorted. 'The only strange thing is why you yourself hadn't investigated this man, after what I told you about the harpoons this morning! I assume you're being paid good money to solve crimes, Inspector. Then why ignore the only clue you actually had? Who knows — under police interrogation, this fellow Gregory might have been afraid and divulged the name of the man who stole those harpoons! It's clear to me that the phantom, whoever he may be, realised we were investigating the weapons, and knew he'd been seen taking them by Gregory. He must also have known that after that first killing, it wouldn't take Gregory long to put two and two together and get the right answer! So he had to dispose of him!'

'There you go again, theorising,' snarled Bristol. 'I don't suppose you did have anything to do with the murders — you've got witnesses to say you didn't in each case — but you've been poking that long nose of yours into the affair after I had expressly forbidden you to do so!'

'*You* had forbidden me to do so? And who, may I ask, do you imagine you are, to have any right to forbid anyone making an effort to solve a murder case?'

He selected a further matchstick from

the ashtray and grunted: 'I'm warning you, Morland, you'll be getting involved too deeply in this case! I can make things very unpleasant for you!'

'Look here, Bristol,' I returned just as rudely, 'I'll give you one last tip, since you seem unable to think for yourself. Put a guard on Leslie Stomberoff, the actor! Do it now! How do we know he didn't see something also?'

'Nonsense. I've questioned all the workmen who took down the house and took out the furniture. None of them saw anything!'

'Probably not! But remember, most of the time they were busy inside the house, whereas Stomberoff and Gregory were outside, looking on!'

'I'm asking you again to mind your own business, Morland! It's a hundred to one that this idiot Stomberoff saw nothing!'

'That may be, but the phantom doesn't know — he *can't* know for sure — whether Stomberoff saw him or not! Perhaps he'll kill Stomberoff to make sure!'

'Poppycock,' sneered Bristol. 'I tell you, Morland, lay off! If it'll satisfy you, I'll have

Stomberoff questioned tomorrow. But in the meantime, be good enough to keep your nose out of this!'

I flushed angrily and turned to Angela. 'Let's be getting home,' I said shortly. 'If we stay round here much longer, we'll be driven as simple as the inspector!'

'Here, wait a minute,' boomed Bristol. 'I didn't say you could leave yet!'

'No? What else do you want us for? You've taken our statements, our fingerprints, our footmarks.'

'Very well, you can go. But don't leave the district!'

'Of course not! I'd hate to miss the opportunity of seeing the events that are going to reduce you to the ranks! I'll stick around, don't worry!'

A stout uniformed constable suddenly panted in. His flushed face and gulping breathing pointed to the fact that he had been running hard. He gasped: 'He's dead, sir!'

'I know he's dead, you blasted fool,' roared Bristol. 'He was dead when I got here! Think I'm blind?'

'No, sir … I mean the man we've just found!'

'What?' Bristol shot to his feet like someone who had just squatted on a clump of holly.

'Yes, sir — we found another of them, just along the street. He's had his stomach ripped open with one of them 'arpoons! Lumme, it was awful!'

'Who is it?' bellowed Bristol. 'Who *is* it, man?'

'It's that idiot, sir — you know, the fellow who isn't what you might call with us. That actor, Leslie Stomberoff!'

Bristol looked as if he would drop through the floor at any moment. His mouth opened and his eyes closed, as if he were reeling off a silent prayer.

I said sweetly: 'Er — bit too late to question Stomberoff, isn't it, Bristol? Perhaps if you'd listened to an *amateur*, you'd have got somewhere before the poor devil was slaughtered! Well — too bad! Good night, Inspector.'

He made no move to detain us as we walked out. Once outside we walked home rapidly, not speaking much. Angela said: 'Poor Stomberoff! He never harmed anyone!'

I nodded silently in agreement. 'It's evident that this phantom is flesh and blood,' I remarked at length. 'Otherwise, why all the haste to eliminate those who might have been able to have pinned something on him? If I were Bristol, I'd also have a close watch kept on those workmen who were there at the time the harpoons vanished. But of course, you can't tip Bristol off to anything without getting your head bitten off!'

We paused for a few minutes in the garden of Walter's home while Angela composed herself. She shuddered in the cold wind, and I placed a comforting arm about her. The perfume from her hair drifted up and into my nostrils, and a stray tendril brushed against my face. Then, only half aware of what I was doing, I swung her into my arms, pressed her against me, and brought my lips full down onto hers. They were soft beneath mine, slightly parted. I felt her body stiffen against the embrace; then suddenly she wasn't fighting anymore. She clung to me, her arms went about my neck, and she returned my kiss with interest.

I don't know how long we stood like that, pressed close against each other. It was a momentary way of escape from the horrors that continually surrounded us, and we took full advantage of it. For a short, sweet period, we shut out the harshness of realities and possibilities; and there, in that dead, wintry garden on Charnel Estate, we found a world in which nothing existed except two sets of lips pressed together, and two bodies which clung so tightly that they might have been one, and two hearts which thumped at the awareness of that physical contact.

Then it was over; and breaking apart, we turned and went up the steps to the house. Neither of us spoke; neither of us could trust ourselves to speak. But I knew that if Angela had only been amusing herself, I had not! I knew that she possessed that indescribable something which, for me, no other woman had possessed. And I wondered, vaguely, if she felt it too.

I think we both looked slightly guilty as we told Walter and Annabelle of the two murders. Bob, a hard worker during the day, had already retired, so the four of us sat round the fire and recounted our exploits of the evening. It seemed that Walter also had something to tell. He had received a phone call from a London estate agent, asking him if he would care to sell the Charnel Estate, and offering him an absurdly low price. He had, needless to say, refused; but when I broke my news, his face fell and he said: 'This is the last straw, Wenton! I must sell or I'll be able to get nothing back!'

'You mean that after this more workers than ever will go?'

'Naturally. I'd be the very last to expect them to stay on in a place where they might be murdered at any time.'

I said nothing in reply, but I asked him for the address of the estate agent who had contacted him. 'I'm going to London first thing in the morning,' I said. 'But while I'm gone, I want you to promise to do nothing rash! Don't clinch the sale of the estate — wait until I get back.'

'All right. It can't do any harm to hold on a while longer.'

And so we left it for the time being.

* * *

The secretary admitted me to a shabby inner office, and I eyed the gross, fleshy-looking man behind the desk. 'Mr. Holms? The estate agent?'

'I am Mr. Holms, yes. What can I do for you? Are you interested in any property?'

'I am, rather. Yes, I am extremely interested in property.'

He rubbed his hands and drew a sheet of paper towards him. 'A fashionable home, sir? Was that what you wanted?'

I shook my head. 'I'm not interested in anything of that nature — nothing that you have on your books, Mr. Holms. I'm interested in an estate! Perhaps you've heard of it? The Charnel Estate?'

An expression of shifty cunning crossed his features. I went on: 'I have reasons for desiring to obtain that particular patch of ground.'

'And you want me to handle the deal for you?'

'That's about it, Mr. Holms.'

'Well, let me see now. There seems to be quite a market for the Charnel Estate! I have a client who also wants that particular property. Of course, it isn't goin' to be easy to get hold of it; but with that haunting business going on there, there's a chance that the owner might sell out — if the price was right! Now, my other client has offered me fifty percent of the purchase price. That is, whatever I buy for, he will give me an additional fifty percent. He seems very anxious to get hold of the ground; but if you could make me a better offer, sir, I would communicate with you first.'

'This other client,' I said, trying to appear only slightly interested, 'perhaps I know him? What is his name?'

I must have put it rather too bluntly, for Holms's lips shot into a tight, thin line. 'It isn't *ethical* to divulge the identity of my clients.'

'I realise that, but you can understand my natural desire to know who I'm up against. Now if this would help ...' I casually extracted a ten-pound note from my wallet, and his eyes followed it as I laid it on his desk.

At length he said: 'Ah! Well, of course, there isn't any reason why I should keep the gentleman's name a secret. I've never seen him, but he signs his letters Michael Rook. He has so far only communicated with me by letter.'

This stumped me utterly. I had heard a number of names mentioned since I had arrived at the estate, but I knew no one by the somewhat unusual name of Michael Rook. Though if my fancies were correct, the man, whoever he was, would hardly have given his real name.

'Hmm,' I said thoughtfully. 'Perhaps you'd be good enough to permit me to see one of his letters?'

Holms shook his head decisively. 'I can't go that far, Mr.—er —?'

'Jones,' I supplied. 'Frank E. Jones.'

'Mr. Jones. I haven't any objection to telling you that the letters were posted from the Charnel Estate itself.'

This followed my own reasoning. 'And you have no idea why this — er — Rook wishes to secure the estate?'

'No more idea than I have why *you* wish to secure it.'

'I see. I suppose he is prepared to pay well?'

'Confidentially, he has named a sum that quite surprised me, seeming to be far too much for a piece of haunted property. I take it that you will, if necessary, go above the amount he named?'

'Might I know the amount?'

'Twenty-five thousand pounds as a starting figure; to run up, if necessary, to fifty.'

I picked up my hat, and he bustled to open the door for me. 'Quite a large sum for a piece of property on which no one will care to reside,' I told him. 'And one which I am not prepared to better! I'm sorry, but we can't do business, Mr. Holms. Good day, sir.'

'But — but —' he gasped. And then I had left the outer office and was walking quickly down the stairs.

My visit had not revealed as much as I had hoped, but it had convinced me that someone wanted the Charnel property. That, apparently, was the whole of the rhyme and reason behind the phantom of Charnel Estate!

6

The Last of Bristol

I arrived back early in the afternoon and immediately went for a long walk, not omitting any portion of the estate from my tour. For hours I was no nearer to arriving at a solution of the mystery; and then, on a large bare patch of ground on which many children were at play, I found something that interested me deeply. It was a piece of translucent, brittle stuff, and I stowed it carefully away in my pocket and returned to Walter's home. Here I made it into a parcel and registered and dispatched it from the local post office.

It was directed to a friend of mine in London, an analytical chemist, with instructions to rush me a report of the analysis. There was little more I could do now for the time being, so I took a walk as far as the factory, and went into Walter's office to have a word with him. He was looking pale and drawn; much more depressed than when I had arrived.

As I entered, he took his head from between his hands and said: 'It's no good, Wenton. I'll have to accept that agent's offer of twenty thousand pounds!'

'You'll do nothing of the kind,' I told him firmly. 'In the first place, that agent is willing to go as high as fifty thousand — and even that, if my opinion is correct, would be merely a hundredth part of the value of this estate!'

He gazed at me bemusedly.

'I don't wish to say any more at the moment, in case I am wrong. But whatever you do, Walter, hold on until the day after tomorrow!'

'If you say so, Wenton. But I can't see any reason for holding on. The factory is behind with contracts already, and I'll be sued for every penny I have for failing to fulfil them. Exactly one hundred and fifty men tendered their resignations this morning. Some of them would have stayed, I expect, but their wives wouldn't. You see the jam I'm in, Wenton! It's hellish!'

'I still advise you to hold out — I feel confident that I'll have some good news for you soon.' He shook his head; but when I left a while later, he agreed to do as I asked.

I made my way next to the local police station and enquired where I might contact Detective-Inspector Bristol. As luck would have it, he was actually on the spot; and in the small room, with a curious sergeant looking on, I proceeded to inform him of my visit to London.

'So it's my opinion,' I concluded, 'that if you get the man so anxious to buy Charnel, you'll get the phantom! I suggest you have this agent questioned, to see if you can find out any more than I did.'

'Morland,' he told me, after I had finished, 'I've stood about all the interference I'm going to from you! I'm sick and tired of damned amateurs trying to tell me what and what not to do! As for this story of yours, it's fantastic, man!'

'Perhaps you can think of a better motive, then?'

'I admit I can't at the minute. But to suggest that anyone would repeatedly murder strangers to gain a piece of land such as this is a bit too far-fetched for my liking!'

'Suppose the land were valuable property?'

'How can it be?'

'There are such things as mineral deposits.'

He clutched at his brow in mental anguish and snorted: 'Go away, Morland, *please* go away! I'm having a bad enough time with this case without you tangling the lines and making it worse! I'm here to find out who killed who, not whether this ground is valuable!'

'But — you idiot,' I said in exasperation, 'can't you see that what I have said supplies a *motive*?'

'I don't want to hear your crazy motives! Will you stop bothering me, and butting into things that are not your concern!'

I went; there was little else I could do. Undoubtedly, Detective-Inspector Bristol was the most stupid, obstinate, self-opinionated man I had ever come across.

I was reading a book in the drawing room when Angela came in and flung herself into the chair opposite me. I told her about my trip to London in answer to her questions, and she nodded in agreement when I explained that it was my opinion the Charnel Estate was valuable ground.

Dinner that night was a very gloomy meal; my own mind was on that specimen which I had sent to London, and Bob and Walter were glumly discussing the situation at the factory. Annabelle and Angela retired soon after dinner to Angela's room to chat, as women do; and shortly after they had gone, Bob rose also, yawned, stretched, and said: 'I think I'll turn in now, Walter. Good-night. Good-night, Wenton!'

I replied rather absent-mindedly, and he swung off up the stairs. I sat on with Walter, talking over those days at Cambridge, and for a while we both managed to forget our worries in cheerful reminiscing.

Then Walter went to his study to attend to some business papers, and I got up, donned hat and coat, and went for a stroll. The moon was covered by dense masses of cloud; a contrast to the previous night, I thought as I strolled the lonely roads. And a perfect night for the phantom to put in a spot of work!

I walked as far as the Charnel Arms and stopped off for a drink. Much to my surprise, the place was deserted, save for the landlord, who was leaning mournfully on the counter, his head between his hands. As I entered, he started up and made a grasp for a long-handled, keen-bladed axe which reposed beside him; but as he saw who it was, he heaved a sigh of relief and replaced the weapon.

'Afraid I might have been the phantom?' I asked with a smile in which there was little mirth.

He poured me a whisky and said: 'And haven't I a right to be?'

'I suppose you have! I see by that axe that you aren't going to be caught napping!'

'Not I. I'm a bit jittery, I suppose; but if that damned thing comes in here, he'll get what he's looking for!'

'Good for you. Join me?'

'I don't mind. It's pleasant to see a face here again. The minute darkness falls, they all go slinking off home — but me, I've got to stay here and keep this pub open until ten o'clock! It's a bit hard, sir. And my old woman went off to Portsmouth yesterday

— said she wouldn't stop another minute in the Charnel Estate. So I'm by way of being a bit lonely, you see.'

'I see. The phantom certainly has frightened people from going out after dark!'

'Blimey,' said the man, glancing towards the door, 'here's another customer! Well, things are picking up! We'll be crammed out if it goes on like this!'

I turned to see who had come in, and my gaze met that of Detective-Inspector Bristol. He was looking more subdued than usual, and he even went so far as to nod pleasantly to me. He leaned on the bar beside me, and in reply to my cordial invitation, replied that he would have a double whisky and splash. When this was set before him, he twiddled the glass aimlessly for a moment, then said: 'I've been thinking over your theory, Morland, and I find there might be something in what you say after all. If I was a little bit pig-headed this morning, you must forgive me. All these murders are getting on my nerves, you know.'

It was a most handsome apology, coming from a man like Bristol, and I said, pleasantly: 'Forget it, Inspector. All I wish to do is to help you. I'm not trying to step in and take any credit for solving the mystery. I don't give a damn who solves it, as long as these killings are nipped in the bud!'

'Then perhaps we can work together?'

'Of course. If I find out anything of value, I'll let you know at once.'

'Good! And meanwhile I'll ask the Yard to have this agent you mentioned questioned.'

'Have you any line yourself on this phantom?' I asked.

'Nothing of value — except that I know he *isn't* a phantom, for certain!'

'You do?'

'It was the footprints. You remember last night when we took impressions of yours and your lady friend's? Well, we found three fresh sets of prints outside Gregory's back door: yours, the lady's, and one other set, which had been made by rubber soles — probably on soft pumps. I think that proves the phantom is quite human!'

'It does indeed. I thought so all along, but this makes it certain!'

'It's still a mystery, though. You say you pumped three bullets directly into the phantom?'

'I'm sure they must have hit him, yes.'

'And we didn't find any spent bullets lying behind the house! But how the devil did the man manage to walk away with three bullets in him? Answer that! And not only walk away, but in addition, commit a second murder! It's unbelievable!'

'Not exactly, Inspector. There is such a thing as bullet-proof attire. I should think the phantom wouldn't be likely to neglect the risk of being fired at — I'm convinced he was wearing some kind of vest which prevented the shots from penetrating. Remember, I saw him momentarily waver as the bullets struck him. That would be the force of the impact which made him stagger!'

'In that case, should I ever meet up with him, I'll remember your tip and fire for his head, not his body!'

He took his leave shortly afterwards, saying he was going to take a look round the estate before returning to the station.

I remained for a time talking to the landlord; and when I finally left, the time was half-past nine by my wristwatch. I strolled easily back towards Walter's place, keeping my wits on the alert in case I should bump into the phantom. Once I thought I saw a shadow move ahead of me, and my heart leapt into my mouth. But it proved to be merely a black cat, and I went on my way, feeling somewhat foolish at my own imaginary terrors.

Perhaps this episode had made me less careful. Whatever it was, I failed to hear any sound until a moment before I was struck on the head! Then I heard a soft padding step, and immediately after I felt a violent blow against the back of my neck, and I pitched forward onto my face.

I don't suppose I really lost consciousness, which was where the phantom made his mistake. For as I lay there, stunned, but still able to see and hear and feel, I felt myself turned upwards; saw that ghastly leering face above me; heard that obscene, chuckling laughter; and beheld the harpoon-shaped weapon in the phantom's grasp, raised, ready to strike ...

Death had never been so close to me. My eyes riveted upon that dreadful weapon, my mouth suddenly dry. I lay there, waiting for the stroke …

It came, flashing downwards … and with a superhuman effort of will, I rolled hastily to one side. I heard the ring of the metal harpoon as it struck the pavement; then I had reached my knees, from which position I flung myself at the spectre.

I made contact at thigh-level, and anything less like a ghost to the touch I had never felt: he was as solid as any human being. Taken off his guard — for he had assumed I was senseless — he staggered sideways and almost fell. Then he observed my hand emerging with the gun gripped in it, and turning hastily he made off down the road at a speed which, if I had been an athletic manager, would have made me sign him up to run at Olympia for any figure he named.

I myself was still on my knees, but I raised my gun and pumped the trigger frantically. Nothing happened, and I cursed as I realised the safety catch was still on. I shot it back, but by the time I had done so, the phantom was no longer to be seen. He had gone, leaving his weapon lying beside me on the ground.

Still feeling a trifle dizzy, I slowly got to my feet and explored my aching head with tentative forefingers. I could detect no break in the skin, and heaving a sigh of relief, I bent and picked up the harpoon which the ghoul had dropped. My fingers felt wet and sticky as I touched it, and a pang of horror crossed my mind. I peered closely and noticed a darkish stain on the handle. Blood! The phantom had had blood on his hands! Which could only mean one thing: that I was not his first victim tonight, and that with the other — or *others*—he had met with more success!

I deliberated whether to carry on to Walter's or to head back to the police station and acquaint Bristol with the facts. I decided that I might as well carry on to the house and phone in a report from there. The moon was still lurking beneath layers of cloud when I turned into the street leading to Walter's home. I was moving hurriedly, almost running, for I had no desire to bump into that fiend again before I had at least fortified myself with a double whisky or a spot of brandy.

In the darkness, my flying feet stumbled against something soft; and it was only by an effort that I retained my balance. A premonition made me tremble as I shone my torch down on the obstacle ... and a gasp tore from my bone-dry throat as I saw in the torch beam the dead, staring eyes of Detective-Inspector Bristol!

7

What Weyland Saw

Bristol!

He had been lying there for some time, as the dark stains under him testified. His eyes were panicky — or had been — but they were now assuming a fish-like glaze. The harpoon jutted from his stomach at a peculiar angle; and once again it was clear that the weapon had been repeatedly driven home, wrenched out of the quivering flesh, and driven home again, to ensure a reasonably quick death. There was an additional pool of blood behind his head, and as he had squirmed onto his side in his pain, I could see that his hair at the back was clotted with blood. Seemingly he had been struck down from behind as I had, only he had not been so fortunate!

I left him there, as there was little else I could do, and dashed to Walter's. Within a few minutes I was on the phone to the local police sergeant; and he, horrified, agreed to hasten along at once with an ambulance.

All was quiet and deserted in the house, and it was with some trepidation that I reluctantly went back to the corpse without rousing anyone. Bristol was still there, lying as I had left him, and I sat down on a low wall and lit up my pipe in an effort to still the jumping of my nerves. My hand rested on the revolver in my pocket — I was taking no more chances!

I don't suppose it would have been more than a few minutes before the ambulance, bearing the sergeant, came purring along, but to me it seemed an illimitable eternity. The sergeant, looking very shocked and somewhat nervous, took my statement; and in a short while the ambulance was rolling off, again bearing the sergeant with it. I had thought he would have made a search of the neighbourhood to see if any clues had been left, but obviously he either thought this unnecessary or he was too unnerved to undertake the job.

As I returned to Walter's, I was thinking how strange it was that I should have stumbled across every body save that of Stomberoff. It seemed that my mission in life had become to detect murders—*after* they had been committed.

I found Walter in the hall, gazing out of the door along the street. He was clad in pyjamas and a dressing gown, and seemed rather anxious. When I rolled in his face lit up, and he said: 'Thank heavens you're all right! I heard someone dash in here, use the phone, and run out again. I got up to see what was wrong, and I heard the sound of a car. When I looked out I could see the red ambulance sign on the front of it. I thought that something had happened to you, old chap; in fact, I was just about to slip some clothes on when the ambulance drove away. What on earth's been going on?'

'Pretty ghastly business,' I told him in a subdued tone. 'The phantom's been at it again!'

'Good God! Where — when — who was it this time?'

'Bristol,' I told him. 'Just down the road here. It's a wonder you didn't hear him scream — but then, perhaps he didn't scream at all. He wasn't the type of man to, no matter what hell he was going through. Poor old Bristol!'

Shaking his head sadly, Walter retired soon after. I sat on for a few minutes, smoking a thoughtful pipe. Then, my mind weary and strained, I went along to my room.

As I have said before, my room was on the ground floor, and next door to it was the room that Angela occupied. It was as I was treading — as I thought, quietly — past her room that I heard her voice calling to me.

'Wenton . . .'

I stopped and went over to the closed door.

She called again, softly: 'Is that you, Wenton?'

'It is.'

'Come in a minute, will you?'

I hesitated. I suppose I have always been a stickler, more or less, for the proprieties; and as much as I thought of Angela, it was hard to shake off the ingrained sense of decorum that I considered fitting. For a guest, under a friend's roof, to be found in the bedroom of that friend's sister-in-law late at night, was unthinkable to me. But, as I have already recorded, Angela was one of those modern women, perfectly well able to look after herself, and inclined to turn a blind eye to conventionalities. So, after a moment's pause, I turned the handle silently and went in. As a gesture to the gods of propriety, I left the door half open, and having satisfied my conscience in this way, I moved over to Angela's bed.

She looked beautiful, almost unearthly, in the rose-tinted glow of the bed lamp. She was sitting propped up against her pillow, a discarded book lying by her side, and a worried look on her small, delicate features. Her thin nightdress revealed the wonders of the upper portion of her figure, and I found myself feeling pleased that, although she was a 'modern woman', she did not despise the nightdress in favour of pyjamas. Her hair was loose and fell upon her bare white shoulders, and her lips were parted; her eyes were rather drowsy, but as I came across they sought mine.

'Has anything been happening, Wenton?'

'Nothing that can't wait until tomorrow,'

I told her, not wishing to disturb her slumber with my grisly story.

'You — haven't been in any trouble or anything?'

'Good lord, of course not!' I laughed. 'What makes you think I have?'

'I heard someone come rushing in … and then I heard Walter come down the stairs calling your name. I almost got up and came to see.'

'You were worried?'

'Terribly worried. Do you think, after what happened last night, that I wouldn't be?'

I was silent a moment, hardly knowing what to say. Then I smiled and told her lightly: 'You mean in the garden? But I wasn't sure if you were just flirting with me, Angela. I thought you might have been carried away by the strain and the circumstances.'

'Is *that* what you were?' she cut in quickly.

'No! I'll be frank with you, Angela. I think I loved you from the moment I saw you.'

'And didn't you know, when we kissed last night, that I felt the same? Do you think I'd kiss any man like that purely and simply from a desire to flirt?'

'I was a fool,' I told her. 'I should have known that it wasn't just another casual kiss. I'm sorry, Angela.'

She smiled and patted the bed by her side. 'Sit down a minute, Wenton.'

'Do you think I should? I mean, it's late, and it isn't the done thing. Suppose someone should —'

'Are you frightened of ruining your reputation?' she teased.

'Of course not. I was thinking more of you!'

'Then don't! Who cares what other people think, as long as we know everything's all right? Please sit down, Wenton, and tell me just what happened to you tonight.'

Not without some misgiving, I sat down. There was nothing wrong in that, of course, but what I was afraid of was myself. The temptation of seeing Angela so near, and so lovely, was almost more than I could resist. In order to take my mind off her, I told her quietly about Bristol's death, and how I myself had sustained a nasty crack on the head. She was horrified at the news of poor Bristol, and her eyes clouded over.

'Oh, Wenton, when will it be all over? Will it ever be?'

'I can't tell you that, Angela,' I said. 'But if this sample I sent to London proves to be what I suspect, then automatically the motive for the crimes will be uncovered. From there it will be only a step to investigating that crooked estate agent, and that should put the police on the killer's trail.'

'But how about Walter? He'll lose a fortune if he has to sell the estate.'

'I know — but if the specimen proves on analysis to be the stuff I suspect, he won't *want* to continue with the factory and estate. He'll make a hundred times as much from this ground as he could with the factory, believe me!'

'I'm so glad to hear that. Walter's awfully nice, and I've been almost as worried as Anna about this affair. Besides, I have to thank him for the opportunity of meeting you!'

'That's another thing,' I told her. 'We have the phantom to thank, also. But for him we should never have met — I don't suppose I'd ever have come down here at all.'

'I'm glad you did,' she said softly. 'I don't want to lose you again, ever.'

I struggled with an uncomfortable feeling in my throat, then I said earnestly: 'Angela, I want to — to — ask you something.'

'Yes, Wenton?'

'Look here, Angela — I love you more than I've ever loved anyone or anything in my entire life, and I know I'll go on loving you . . . will you marry me, dear?'

She was silent, her eyes cast down, her fingers plucking at the eiderdown.

I stammered: 'I know it isn't a very dashing proposal . . .'

'I thought it was beautiful, darling,' she said softly.

'And . . .?'

'You're certain you really want me?'

'I was never so certain of anything. I know it's sudden and all that . . . and I know I've only known you a few days. But that's long enough for me to know exactly how much I love you. Of course, if you think I'm rushing things —'

'I don't think you're rushing things, Wenton, dear. As a matter of fact, I've been looking forward to this since the day you arrived. Even then, I felt something when I looked at you.'

'Then you will marry me?'

'Of course I will, silly! Let anybody try and stop me!'

And then the magic of her beauty overpowered my better judgment, and my arms were about her, my lips caressing her cheeks and shoulders; and she pressed her lips against my forehead and sighed with contentment.

'I beg your pardon!'

The voice came from the direction of the half-opened doorway, which we had both forgotten. I hastily released Angela from my arms, and flushing furiously, turned to face Bob Weyland, who was standing in the doorway. He was clad in pyjamas and a dressing-gown, and his hair was tousled as if he had been sleeping recently. But there was no trace of sleep in his face. It was red, and in that moment, furious. His eyes shot hate towards us, and his hands were lightly clenched by his sides.

'Bob!' gasped Angela. 'How dare you pry into other people's business?'

'*Other people's business?*' he sneered bitterly. 'I think, considering I am *engaged* to you, that this *is* my business!'

'You're not engaged to me, Bob! You never were! That was something you took for granted—*too* much for granted! I never gave you any reason to believe I would marry you!'

'I admit that. But you never bothered to disillusion me, did you? You let me go on thinking —'

'I didn't want to hurt your feelings, Bob.'

'You've hurt them now, haven't you? Damn you, how do you think I feel, knowing you're just a cheap slut who'd let any man in her bedroom?'

He got no further. I was off the bed, and my fist, with all my force behind it, crashed into his enraged face. He flew backwards, cannoned against the passage wall, and crashed to the floor. He was still lying where he fell, and I bent over him as Angela joined me.

'He'll be all right,' I told her. 'I'm sorry this has happened. We were rather careless.'

'It doesn't matter,' she said, her voice trembling. 'It was my fault for calling you into my room … but I hadn't any idea Bob felt so strongly about me. Why, he wasn't ever so possessive before, and he was engrossed with his work. He hardly ever took me out or tried to make love to me. Perhaps if he had, we'd have had this out a long time ago. Is he hurt?'

But I failed to answer her remark. For I had opened Bob's gown and pyjama top to give him air, and my eyes fell on his chest. I felt the blood roaring in my ears as I gazed down at him. I half hoped I was seeing things, and I shut my eyes; but when I reopened them those tell-tale marks were still visible.

Angela was looking at me strangely, and as if from far away I heard her voice saying: 'Wenton, darling, are you all right? Wenton!'

I shook myself and replied that I was. Then I pointed to the three circular-shaped blue bruises on Bob Weyland's chest. 'You remember me firing three shots at the phantom that night at Gregory's place?' I said.

Her eyes widened and she nodded.

'I took it for granted that the phantom was wearing some kind of bullet-proof vest.'

Again she nodded without speaking.

'If he was,' I continued, 'it is certain that the bullets would — although prevented from penetrating — have bruised his flesh badly … and Bob Weyland here has three bruises in the spot where those bullets of mine must have hit the phantom!'

As the full implication of what I was saying hit her, she almost reeled; she stared down at the senseless surveyor, her eyes almost starting from her head. 'It can't be — surely — not Bob! He — he isn't capable of anything like that!' she whispered.

'If I read that look on his face rightly when he found us together, he's capable of anything,' I said grimly.

'But — Wenton, we can't be sure. There are a hundred ways he could have obtained those bruises … we daren't jump to any conclusions …'

'I've an idea,' I told her. 'It'll mean some danger for you, but if you're willing to chance it —'

'I'll chance anything to trap whoever is the killer,' she whispered with a shudder.

Quickly I replaced Weyland's clothing before he regained consciousness. I told Angela to go back into her room; that I would explain in the morning. And then I carried Weyland upstairs, threw him on his bed, and went back to my own room. But I didn't sleep: all night long, I kept a close watch on Weyland's door!

8

The End of the Phantom

We were all at breakfast when Bob Weyland came down late the following morning. I had explained to Walter and Annabelle that Angela and I were engaged, and Walter, although a little taken aback, was enthusiastic in his congratulations. Annabelle, however, seemed only a little surprised, and I guessed that Angela had been telling her a little of her feelings.

Weyland had missed work; I suppose the bump on the head had made him feel a little out of sorts, for his head had struck the wall when I had punched him the previous night. He made no reference to the passage, and it wasn't until after breakfast, when Angela and Annabelle had retired to the kitchen to attend to the cooking of lunch, that he spoke. Walter had hurried down to the factory again immediately after breakfast, and Weyland

and I were alone in the dining-room.

'I'm sorry about what happened last night, Morland,' he said. 'You did right to hit me — I'm afraid I was damned offensive!'

'Forget it,' I told him without much cordiality. 'I'm only too sorry I had to do it!'

'Of course, I haven't any real claim on Angela — but, well, it was rather a shock, and at the time I didn't know you were engaged.'

'It's all right. For my part, I'm sorry I hit you so hard.'

'You had the right to. Actually, you didn't hit me hard enough! I was a fool! I had got up to go down to the drawing-room for my pipe — I couldn't sleep, and I thought a smoke would help me ... I couldn't help seeing what was going on when I passed Angela's room. I don't know what came over me ... it was the shock, I suppose ...'

He sounded genuine enough, but his eyes betrayed his tone. I could see a venomous light in them; a light that would not have been present in the eyes of a contrite man.

He retired to his room soon afterwards, saying he felt a bit seedy; but before doing so, he apologised quite frankly to Angela. He was unaware that we had seen those bruises on his chest; and even if he had known, I doubt if he would have realised how clearly they indicated him as the guilty man.

Soon after lunch, I took Angela aside and explained what I wished her to do that evening. She seemed rather nervous, and I almost decided not to put the plan into operation, but she insisted.

About three o'clock I received a telegram from London. It came from my analytical friend, and was brief, but intriguing:

'Specimen you sent put through exhaustive test. Analysis: pitchblende uranium bearing similar composition to veins discovered at St. Stephens, Cornwall, early this century. Sending specialist down for complete geological survey.

Walmesley.'

So that was the secret of Charnel Estate! A portion of ground, rich in veins of the precious uranium-bearing pitchblende. I had suspected some precious mineral, but nothing like this.

Bob Weyland — if he really was the phantom — was playing his murder game to drive Walter to sell the valuable property for a song. He would purchase it through the estate agent and would quickly resell, or amass a fortune by floating a company to exploit the territory. Obviously he had come across the find while surveying the lie of the land, and, keeping his discovery secret, had set about devising a method of forcing his unsuspecting friend and employer to part with his property. How nearly he had succeeded you can judge for yourselves!

The harpoons — of course Weyland, in charge of the demolition, would have had an excellent chance to filch the weapons. No wonder he retired early each night! Apparently he did this to divert suspicion, and later sneaked down and out of the house to continue his campaign of terror.

But my plan would catch him red-handed! Three bruises on the chest were by no means conclusive proof, and it was essential to procure more evidence than this. I was sure that there would be nothing in his room to point to his guilt; remember, once or twice I had seen him return to the house after the phantom had been on the prowl, and he had not been carrying any parcels, or anything which might have concealed his black attire.

I decided not to mention the telegram to anyone for the time being; if Weyland knew his secret was out, he would probably not think it worthwhile to carry on with the ghost game, and the last chance of catching him in the act would be gone.

I was a great deal disturbed over using Angela as bait, but I didn't see how any harm could come to her, and I assuaged my conscience by telling myself that there could not possibly be any flaw in my plan.

It was, briefly, this: Angela, soon after dinner that evening, was to say she had promised to visit a friend of hers on the other side of the estate. She was to ask me if I would accompany her, and I would complain of tiredness and decline. I would then mention the phantom, and she was to laugh at me and say she didn't think there'd be any chance of her meeting up with that spectre. This was to implant the idea in Bob's mind. Then she was to leave the house, in spite of my protests. It was my hope, after what had occurred the previous night, that Weyland, eager for revenge on the woman who had spurned him, would once again don his phantom garb after sneaking from the house, and attempt to attack and kill Angela. But of course, I should be there to prevent this unpleasant possibility.

Weyland's bedroom window was some thirty feet from the ground, a sheer drop that no man could take repeatedly without injuring himself. Therefore I assumed he must return down the staircase and sneak out by one of the doors. It was my intention to watch that staircase like a hawk; and, when he came, to trail him silently, wait until he had donned his phantom attire, and then catch him red-handed!

Everything went smoothly. The plan was put into effect immediately after dinner by Angela, who said: 'I promised to call on Mary Grey over on Gresom Road. Care to come with me, Wenton?'

'No, I don't think so, Angela. I'm a little

tired. But if I were you, I wouldn't go at all. You know very well what's happening in this place!'

'Pooh! It's far too early yet for any chance of my meeting the nocturnal phantom.'

'Yes, I suppose it is rather early for him to be out.'

'I'll walk you over, Angela,' said Walter, and I cursed silently as I realised we had not anticipated this eventuality, although it was only logical. But Angela played up gamely.

'Oh, it's all right, Walter. You're tired and worried, and I shall be perfectly safe. Why, it's barely getting dark now.'

Walter was about to speak, but I caught his eye and moved my head negatively. He looked puzzled, but he sensed something, and relaxed into his chair. Angela donned her coat and hat, and within another minute was ready to go.

'I think I'll slip off to bed, if you'll all excuse me,' grunted Bob Weyland, and he left the room. We watched him looking after Angela as she went into the night; then he continued up to his room. I closed the room door, but immediately bent and placed an eye to the keyhole.

'What the devil ...?' exploded Walter. I placed a finger to my lips to enjoin silence, and, somewhat amazed, he sat there staring at me. Annabelle was in the kitchen, so she was spared the surprise of seeing my peculiar actions.

Minutes sped by, and still there was no sign of Weyland. I got uneasy, beckoned Walter over, and whispered to him: 'Stick by this keyhole, Walter. If Weyland comes down the stairs, let me know at once — I'll be in the garden. But don't let him see you, for heaven's sake! He'll probably use the rear door.'

I left Walter there and sneaked cautiously out into the garden. Only the glimmer of starlight lit the house, and, looking up at Weyland's window, I could see it was slightly ajar. I couldn't understand this at all; had I been wrong? Surely, if Weyland was the phantom, and if he wished revenge on Angela, now was his chance! If he left it much later, he would be unable to overtake her before she reached her friends.

Or had he already gone? The thought electrified me; and even as it crossed my mind, my foot knocked against some metallic substance lying under the shadow of the great tree I was leaning upon. Rapidly I stooped, and came up holding a square, tubular affair. For a moment my brain refused to function, and then I knew with horrible certainty what I held — a telescopic ladder! A light, collapsible arrangement of steel tubes, fitting neatly into one another so that the whole thing could be folded to no more than a foot or two, and yet which would extend to a height of twenty-five feet or more. Weyland had gone!

I lost my head then, and tearing across the garden I raced out into the roadway and down it in the direction I knew Angela must have taken. My flying feet seemed hardly to touch the pavement, and my breath came in rasping gulps from my throat. I was only dimly aware of the thumping and pounding of my heart as I raced on into the darkness.

Would I be in time?

I was progressing across the patch of ground where I had found the specimen of pitchblende the previous day, when I became aware of a strange sight in front of me, revealed to my eyes by the glimmering starlight. Standing with her face towards me was Angela! Her features were a mask of sheer terror, and her hands were raised pitifully, as if to ward off that dark, grotesque shape which advanced upon her.

The monster was so intent upon his victim that he failed to hear the soft crunch of my feet across the ground, and as his arm came back for the stroke which was to cut into the defenceless woman, I gripped his shoulder and wrenched him violently backwards. He turned and saw me, his face twisted into a mask of malicious rage. Back went his weapon again, for the stroke that would disembowel me if it fell.

Then my gun was in my hand, and this time there was no mistake. It spat orange flame into his face at point-blank range. Two black holes appeared in his forehead, and a third bullet smashed into his mouth.

A shrill, whining noise tore from his throat, then the grisly weapon of destruction slid from his hand and he thudded to the ground after it. He didn't twitch or move; he was completely dead. In another minute my arms were tight about Angela, and she was sobbing on my coat.

It was all so simple now we had caught the fiend at last. It had been easy for him to stoop under the shelter of the lightweight black draperies he had worn; this had given him the needed hunched appearance. His distorted, grinning features were a skin-tight rubber mask painted with phosphorus; and this, when removed, enabled him to give the impression of having vanished entirely into the shadows.

He had left his room and returned, by means of the tubular ladder, and we found the rest of the harpoons lying in a hollow of the tree I had so recently been leaning against.

Of course, Walter was hard hit to think he had been sheltering such a man. But when he heard the news of the analysis of the ground his estate was built on, his gloom evaporated, and it was a merry party that gathered for coffee late that evening at his home.

He and Annabelle were profuse in their gratitude, but I waved their thanks away with an airy hand and a smile. 'You don't have to thank me,' I said, my arm about Angela's slender waist. 'You've done far more for me than I could ever have hoped to do for you!'

'I don't understand,' said Walter. 'What more could we have done for you, Wenton? What's more valuable than the knowledge you own a piece of ground worth a fortune?'

'Only one thing could be more valuable than that, Walter,' I informed him. 'And you've made it possible for me to obtain it.'

'I still don't understand.' He smiled, looking puzzled.

'I do,' I said, and my eyes met those of Angela, and I knew she understood too!

We do hope that you have enjoyed
reading this large print book.

Did you know that all of our titles
are available for purchase?

We publish a wide range of high
quality large print books including:
**Romances, Mysteries, Classics
General Fiction
Non Fiction and Westerns**

Special interest titles available in
large print are:
**The Little Oxford Dictionary
Music Book, Song Book
Hymn Book, Service Book**

Also available from us courtesy of
Oxford University Press:
**Young Readers' Dictionary
(large print edition)
Young Readers' Thesaurus
(large print edition)**

For further information or a free
brochure, please contact us at:
**Ulverscroft Large Print Books Ltd.,
The Green, Bradgate Road, Anstey,
Leicester, LE7 7FU, England.
Tel:** (00 44) **0116 236 4325
Fax:** (00 44) **0116 234 0205**

Other titles in the
Linford Mystery Library:

A FROZEN SILENCE

Arlette Lees

Deputies Frack Tilsley and Robely Danner are called to a remote section of woods outside their small farming community of Abundance, Wisconsin, where a man stands handcuffed and frozen to a tree. As they investigate this brutal murder, a young woman discovers the purse of a missing secretary from nearby Promontory which contains a cryptic diary. Digging deeper, Tilsley and Danner discover common denominators linking several suspects to two murder victims and possibly a third, with the chief of police himself on their list . . .

THE LADY OF DOOM

Gerald Verner

Whispers have reached Scotland Yard of an elusive figure that has appeared on the dark horizon of crime and is making its influence felt. Then the first threatening letter comes, demanding a huge payment, or death for its recipient. The victim goes to the police for protection — only to be promptly murdered. The same graft has been worked by gangsters in Chicago — and now it seems they have arrived in London. As Scotland Yard strives to find the criminal mastermind responsible, so too does a mysterious woman . . . the Lady of Doom!

RENDEZVOUS WITH A CORPSE

Fletcher Flora

The wayward beauty who comes back to her old hometown to titillate her ex-boyfriend (now a married lawyer) and to blackmail her ex-husband is ripe bait for murder. And murder is just what she gets. Suspicion falls heaviest on the old flame: he was at the scene of the crime and out of his legal mind, befuddled by a number of potent cocktails. The police find his explanation incredible; but his wife, believing in his innocence, sets out to pursue an investigation of her own . . .

THE BLACK HUNCHBACK

Gerald Verner

After researching the legend of the treasure of Langley Towers, Sir Owen Langley informs his daughter Pauline that he has discovered the hidden meaning of the doggerel verse left behind by an ancestor as a clue to its hiding place. But then he mysteriously disappears, after rushing out of the house in the middle of the night in his pyjamas! On the same night, the legendary figure of the Black Hunch-back — the sinister family spectre that haunts the Towers and heralds death — is spotted by Pauline on the lawn . . .

THE EMERALD CAT KILLER

Richard A. Lupoff

A valuable cache of stolen comic books originally brought insurance investigator Hobart Lindsey and police officer Marvia Plum together. Their tumultuous relationship endured for seven years, then ended as Plum abandoned her career to return to the arms of an old flame, while Lindsey's duties carried him thousands of miles away. Now, after many years apart, the two are thrown together again by a series of crimes, beginning with the murder of an author of lurid private-eye paperback novels and the theft of his computer, containing his last unpublished book . . .

ANGELS OF DEATH

Edmund Glasby

A private investigator uncovers more than he bargained for when he looks into the apparent suicide of an accountant . . . What secrets are hiding inside the sinister house on the coast of Ireland that Martin O'Connell has inherited from his eccentric uncle . . . A hitherto unknown path appears in the remote Appalachians, leading Harvey Peterson deep into the forest — and a fateful encounter . . . And an Indian prince invites an eclectic group of guests to his palace to view his unique menagerie — with unintended consequences . . . Four tales of mystery and murder.